WHENEVER
A HAPPY THING
FALLS

WHENEVER A HAPPY THING FALLS

Eric M. Johnson

CLOUD HANDS PRESS

Copyright © 2021 by Eric M. Johnson

Printed in the United States of America

First Edition
PUBLISHED BY CLOUD HANDS, INC.

ISBN 978-0-578-78926-2

Library of Congress Control Number 2021931280

Book Design
PRESSLEY JOHNSON DESIGN, CHICAGO

Photographer
CHRISTINA SHIRES

For Margot, the world should be as pretty as you.

And we, who have always thought
of happiness as rising, would feel
the emotion that almost overwhelms us

whenever a happy thing falls

—Rainer Maria Rilke, The Duino Elegies

AT THE LAKE HOUSE

Michigan: Friday, November 2019

10:22 a.m.

Looming over him, a hundred paces up a hill, was his family's lake house, as massive and silent as it has been for all the twenty-two autumns Bale has known it.

His pinstriped shirt and charcoal slacks—Wall Street's prison garb—were wrinkled and smelled of stale champagne and deodorant. His face ached behind a humiliating eye patch. And he hadn't slept in three days.

He looked at his cracked watch.

10:23 a.m.

The mergers and acquisitions "bullpen" at the elite Chicago investment bank Goldman & Coli LLC, where he has worked since graduating college seven months prior, was already humming.

The sound of tires grinding up the driveway

distracted him from endlessly replaying the booze-laced mayhem inside the firm's conference room only hours earlier. The fact that he was caught by the firm's managing partner—a powerful man with close ties to his own father—added to his acute understanding that the trajectory of his entire life would and must be decided in the next thirty-six hours.

He hiked toward the sound and the body of a late '90s Volvo as it came into view. Out stepped a bearded man with dangling arms, an enormous skull and a Parliament cigarette clenched in his teeth. This was Sutton DiPrenzio, Bale's best friend since high school at Chicago's C.W. Loftman School. They had lived together in London during a semester abroad, and were inseparable after graduation, though he had struggled to see Sutton as Bale's life was increasingly sucked into a labyrinth of mind-melting mathematics and pitch book finessing.

"Jesus, son, you look like shit," DiPrenzio called out, his cigarette bouncing in his jaw as he approached.

"Feel like it, too," Bale said.

They hugged.

"So the managing partner catches you, and you, just, left?"

"What could I say?" Bale said. "It happened so fast. There was a big confrontation. Escher stormed off and yelled, 'We'll deal with this tomorrow.' Then I caught the 11:50 p.m. train out here."

Sutton's eyes flared. He seemed to be both straining to believe and celebrating his friend's behavior, a brazen act of career castration and defiance aimed squarely at Bale's father.

"This is probably the most significant thing you've ever done," Sutton said.

Sutton dragged on his cigarette, scratched the stubble on his cheek.

"What are you going to do? Sutton said. "Can you fix it? Apologize to the partners? I can tell you it would be a fucking catastrophe for your father to find out about this from anyone but you."

Bale was flooded by a maelstrom of guilt, anger and possibility. He had brought a war to his doorstep, and now needed to choose which side he was on.

Later, after they spent the afternoon fishing and drinking in the river upstream of town, they returned to the house at sunset and cooked a pickerel in a large fire in a makeshift trench on the beach. They passed a whiskey bottle between them.

As his friend tipped the whiskey, Bale saw the same expression he remembered from the first time he met Sutton as a freshman at Loftman. Sutton had been flanked in an empty hallway by two towering juniors, one squashing Sutton's backpack under his boot while the other had Sutton's collar in his fist: Sutton's head slightly cocked as his lids softly dropped in perfect time over the black whole notes of his pupils. Those who don't know him mistake this look for cockiness, though Bale had learned it revealed Sutton's innate moral clarity twinned with empathy—a combination that takes most people a lifetime to learn.

Bale badly lost the fight after springing to Sutton's defense—the boys had slurred Sutton's black face and planned to beat him for it. Bale's eye socket was purpled by a haymaker he hadn't expected, and his knees crushed into the polished linoleum before a janitor chased the boys off.

Bale was confused by Sutton's response, as he helped him off the floor—"solid timing" instead of "thank you." It was as if Sutton knew, in his stubborn, clairvoyant way, that he'd have an opportunity to return the favor in Bale's future.

The pair was inseparable ever since, though they were different in major ways that never mattered. Bale was an athlete, charismatic and obsessional, with a newscaster's facial symmetry and poise and a thick neck and shoulders rounded like softballs. Sutton, with gangly limbs that gravity seemed to take a special interest in pulling earthward, was the disaffected philosopher, a spirited contrarian with the raw mental horsepower to make him insufferable to those who challenged him, like the high school bullies. He was repulsed by institutions, self-deception, and vainglorious self-improvement, ranging from New Year's resolutions to Sunday confession. If Sutton made it his business disbelieving, Bale clung to movie-screen notions like love, trust, and compassion, though through childhood he only got to practice and understand those virtues through his mother. His father, Bruce, was a verbally intense man filled with ambition that grew more poisonous with his age.

"Will you go back?" Sutton said.

Bale squinted at a fishing boat bouncing on the waves.

"I mean, it's November, aren't you are up for your bonus, what, next June?"

"I got a direct deposit for $42,500," Bale said. "Prorated for a half year. I get the rest June 1."

"*Good Lord*," Sutton said, his eyes flaring at the sum.

Bale pressed his palms into his skull. "I fucked up, man."

Sutton wasn't sure. In his second year of law school at Northwestern, he had ambitions of battling federal prosecutors as a civil rights attorney or public defender. He would never consider entering the world of Wall Street himself, but he understood what had forced Bale there.

"So. What happened last night?" Sutton said.

Bale reached for the whiskey bottle and began the story.

THE BANK

Chicago: March 2019

86th floor of Willis Tower

The office manager of the investment banking firm Goldman & Coli, LLC led Bale Ratcliffe through "the bullpen"—five adjacent cubicles that lead to a large conference room.

Each partitioned cube was identical and personalized only by mounted nameplates, pitch books, a laptop docking station with twin monitors, and acrylic deal plaques, or "tombstones," as they were known.

Bale was led past the cubicles, seeing only briefly the backs of the neat men toiling inside.

Only the first cubicle, where the firm's newest analyst would sit, was empty. And it was inside that cubicle, Bale's dad promised, that his adult life would begin.

A clock on the wall showed the time—6:45 p.m.

It would still be several hours before the men would go home.

Sherry, the office manager, with posture like a fence post and walnut-colored hair curled up like a cat on her head, brought Bale through the bullpen, and along soy milk-colored walls adorned with reproduced oil paintings to the conference room. He took a chair at one end of the table, placed his resume and a yellow legal pad in front of him and choked a pen in his clammy fingers.

His honey-colored hair was darkened by styling cream, his turquoise eyes and scarlet lips strained to remain relaxed. With his navy suit, Bale achieved a look far older than his twenty-two years.

Ignoble, rotund Escher I. Coli, one of two top managing partners at the firm, waddled into the room.

"Thanks for coming in, again," Escher said as they gripped hands.

"Thank you for the opportunity," Bale said.

Escher paused, pressed the conference room intercom. "Sherry, hello? *Sherry?* Yeah can you bring me a grapefruit LaCroix with lots of ice and a lime?" He pivoted his chubby finger from the intercom and pointed at Bale, "Beverage?"

"No, thank you."

"Well let's just get right down to it, then," Escher said, scanning Bale's resume with annoyance. "Why do you want to be an investment banker?"

"I love finance and I want to learn as much as I can about corporations and the strategic decisions their leaders make. I think investment banking is the best way to do that."

"Yeah, but," Escher paused, his eyes squinting in disbelief, "says here you went to *Middlebury*? And majored in *English*?"

"And economics."

"You seem confused about what you want."

Bale wondered to what extent Escher knew the devil's deal that had forced Bale into that conference room.

"Yes, it is true that it took me until the last year of college to figure out what I wanted."

"And what's that?"

Bale recited the script: "I want to learn finance and accounting and deal-making and then go to business school and eventually take over my father's business."

Escher, looking mildly impressed, said, "Can you work hard?"

"I believe that nothing in life is worth having if it isn't achieved through hard work."

"Give me an example."

"Well, I am currently the editor-in-chief of my college newspaper—"

"*Newspaper?*"

"Yes, sir. *Factual* information is the most valuable commodity there is. I work forty or more hours a week on top of being the captain of the soccer team and having a full economics course load."

"What are your two best and your two worst qualities?"

"I would say that my best qualities are that I am resourceful and intelligent. My worst quality is that I am a perfectionist and it causes me sometimes to be too detail-oriented."

Escher nodded, as if he finally approved.

"The analysts here work an average of eight-five hours a week. Do you think you can handle that?"

"Yes, sir."

Sherry glided into the conference room. "Good. Good. Just put it right here, Sherry. Thank you. What is the highest math you have taken?"

"I am currently enrolled in mathematical statistics."

"I was unaware there was any other kind."

Sherry exited.

"You were saying," he squinted at the resume, "Ballon—look, can I just call you *Bale*?"

He remembered his mother, Ruth, calming him down whenever children or harried adults laughed at the dorky rareness of his name. Ruth told him she had searched for months through her favorite novels and plays and epics, finding *ballon* inside an obscure how-to book on ballet. The word for a dancer's ability to appear effortlessly suspended during a leap, an acrobatic feat that required astounding physical and mental strength and poise. He did not know that, at the time she chose it, with him growing inside her belly, that she hoped to empower him with the extraordinary will needed to soar beyond her husband Bruce's toxic grasp.

"Do you know the four traditional methods of financial valuation?" Escher said.

"Market capitalization, comparable transactions, discounted cash flow analysis, and leveraged buyout analysis."

"Well, say you are doing a discounted cash flow analysis—I am sure you are of course aware that DCF analysis discounts future free cash flow projections to eventually arrive at an entity's present value—can you please tell me first what the formula is for the weighted average cost of capital and then how you know what discount rate to use?"

"I do not have the weighted average cost of capital formula memorized, and our professor usually just gives us the discount rate."

Escher stared blankly.

"Ok. What is, oh, 230,462 divided by 17?" Escher said.

Bale looked at his legal pad. Gripped his pen.

"No writing."

"I use a calculator to avoid inaccuracy."

"That's not completely stupid. What is the sum of the numbers 1-25?"

Bale began figuring.

Escher sipped his seltzer, twitched his nose.

"Too long. Fine, no more math. Look, I've had a long day. Tell me a joke that is both funny and not offensive in any way."

Bale thought, smiled. "What do you get when you cross an elephant and a rhino?"

"I don't know, what do you get?"

"'ell-if-I-know!"

Bale chuckled. Escher did not.

"Ok. Let's end on that. Please wait here."

Bale stood, the two shook hands, and Escher left.

Escher meant to close the door but it stopped, slightly ajar. Bale heard him in the corridor, meeting J. Robert Goldman, the other top partner at the firm.

"Yes" Goldman said.

"Seems intelligent, like a hard worker. Blake Schepp from credit suisse—you remember my old roommate, right? Schepp and Bale's father Bruce are close. Schepp had Bale work at his hedge fund last summer."

"Yes," Goldman said.

"On the debit site, he'll require training and his background's also a bit muddled," Coli said.

"Look, I spoke to Bruce. If the kid's focus wasn't there before, it is now. Bruce made sure of that. And we need an analyst to dump on, we've signed new deals, lost Jeff to Lazard—there is just a lot of work to be done and it's going to start cutting deeper into our weekends."

"OK, yes, make him an offer," Escher said. "If he can pick it up in three months, he'll make it."

· · · · ·

Three months later. June 2019

7:23 a.m.

Mike B. McAllister marched through the unlit office wearing Allen Edmonds so finely polished they stood out against the dark room like a car bumper in moonlight. His muscular arms balanced a shouldered Tumi briefcase and a 16-ounce Americano. He walked with a swagger perfected while trading lean hogs at the Chicago Mercantile Exchange, his previous job. His father, a third-generation breeder, ran one of the largest cattle ranches in Alberta, and the trading pit had made McAllister feel like he was in a bunkhouse crowded with people who would otherwise be transient con artists or gamblers. At 26, he secretly applied to University of Chicago's business school and then got a summer associate job at Goldman & Coli. He was determined to finesse himself into a career that promised shiny things that were not cattle chutes or barbed-wire fences.

McAllister dropped his Tumi against the wall of the third cubicle and turned on the desk lamp.

He then docked his laptop and moved to switch on the bullpen's lighting.

"Let there be light."

He saw legs jutting out from the floor of the first cubicle.

"Holy shit!"

He approached the body slowly. It was not inconceivable that an analyst would be dead.

"Bale!?"

He edged closer and kicked a leg. Bale lurched

awake, lumbered upright and rubbed his face.

"Damn, dude, what happened?" McAllister said.

"All-nighter. General Plastics pitch."

"Fuck."

"Yeah."

Bale stood up and took a deep pull of McAllister's coffee.

McAllister laughed as Bale tucked his wrinkled cotton shirt into his slacks and smoothed his hair.

They reentered their respective cubicles to begin work.

7:45 a.m.

"What's up, you pussies?" Martin R. Fredericks said as he moved quickly past the cubicles holding his iPhone at eye height, swiping through emails. The light from his screen glowed over his pockmarked face and tawny hair, parted sensibly over the peak of his small cranium.

Fredericks was an associate, the mid-level managers between Bale-level analysts and deal-cutting vice presidents. With blond hair a half-inch off his scalp, steel-blue eyes and pockmarks from adolescent acne, Fredericks had the look of a NASA mission control technician from the 1970s, though he was just one generation removed from Dubuque white trash. He was competent, lean and rational, and had survived at Goldman & Coli long enough to earn a deep well of confidence and a $275,000 salary, not counting a massive annual bonus.

"Wait, wait, don't tell me," Fredericks said almost inaudibly as he crept up to J. B. Rothkauf's cube. "Rothkauf's not here yet! *Jesus Christ*, if you ever want to not work, his cubicle is the place to do it."

They roared.

"*He didn't even take his computer home,*" Fredericks noted before moving on to his own cubicle, docking his laptop and clicking open an Excel model. "Ten times a day people stop by to ask me where J. B. is," he mumbled.

For a time, their movements—the pattering of keyboard keys, the shuffling of papers, the searching for an item in a pile, the whispering into the phone, lavish soles rubbing the plush carpeting—cut through the sterile silence.

8:49 a.m.

J. B. Rothkauf strutted into the bullpen in pleated khakis and a peach bowtie. His beat-up suede briefcase hung off his shoulder and his fingers gingerly wrapped an unlidded Earl Grey tea.

"Morning, gentlemen," he said as he strolled by, his face almost always on the edge of a smile.

It took Bale several weeks to learn Rothkauf's strange biography. Rothkauf was not just a South-ern-bred good ol' boy but also a genius who could write computer code by the time he was eleven. At twenty-four, Rothkauf aced the GMAT without preparation.

These facts were unearthed when Rothkauf forgot to remove a MENSA pin from the lapel of his herringbone sport coat and Bale idly asked about it during a team lunch. Rothkauf was then grilled by McAllister.

Bale saw in two months' time that Rothkauf had by far the worst work ethic of any analyst in the history of both analysts and work. But his father had altered his trust agreement to say that his son must graduate college and be continuously employed to thirty-seven years of age before assuming control of the trust.

At twenty-eight, Rothkauf was too old to be an analyst. He got started late in banking by doing research for a biomedical start-up for two years, and then by getting his M.B.A. from University of Chicago for two. He took a job in investment banking—"Because, why not?" he explained—he needed to make it only nine more years to gain control over his millions.

Rothkauf entered Bale's cube. They gave each other a fist bump.

"Wow, you look like hell," Rothkauf said. "Where'd you drink?"

"If by drink, you mean making edits to the General Plastics pitch all night, then, yes, I got ripped," Bale said, handing him the industry overview slides. Rothkauf scanned them. "Escher had me add three new slides and kill the one with the competitor data which I had spent nine hours gathering info for."

"Shit. Well, it's done."

Rothkauf turned to leave and found Fredericks standing in his way, gesturing to the clock, "Only a half day today, J. B. Money?"

"HA HA HA, you bastard. Lake Shore Drive was awful."

Fredericks returned to his cube and J. B. entered his own.

"Hard to get an honest day's work out of anyone these days," Fredericks said.

They eventually shuffled back to their desks and their work, typing, chair sliding, cabinet shutting, the tossing of bounded documents into heaps, the picking up of stuttering phone lines, the checking of emails and voicemails and text messages.

As the clock approached 9 a.m., the work pace increased for everyone, except Rothkauf, who leisurely scanned ESPN and at one point adjusted the mounted birthday cards tacked to the wall of his cubicle. Bale frantically fed a confidentiality agreement into a scanner.

9 a.m.

Escher I. Coli and J. Robert Goldman, the bank's top managing partners, walked in procession to the conference room, with its sprawling mahogany table, oil paintings, and single potted plant. The bullpenners followed the suits.

9:01 a.m.

Goldman's tangerine Hermès tie swayed as he tucked a piece of wintergreen gum into his mouth and scanned the emails Sherry had printed for him on egg-shell printer paper.

The room was quiet while everyone wrote on his legal pad or phone the tasks for the week. Bale's list had twenty-two bullet points.

"OK, let's get started," Goldman said in his booming voice, wisps of thin grey hair dancing slightly in the manufactured office air. "The only thing to report on my end is that I received an email this morning from Landy's CFO. They want to go ahead with the buy-side work."

Goldman paused to let Sherry bring a tray of coffee and bagels to the table. She moved quickly, feeling overcaffeinated eyes locked on her backside as she strained to set down the tray. After she left, Escher was alone in reaching for a bagel.

Goldman continued. "Good work to our team. Martin and Bale, well done. OK, let's go around."

Escher spoke first, in a voice that sputtered like an over-oiled lawnmower, while he struggled to spread a slab of cream cheese evenly across his bagel. The lack of poise visibly horrified Fredericks, who was staring at him.

"We will be meeting with the board of directors at Preo-Mori, a hospice company, on Friday at their of-fices to discuss a possible sale. Five hundred million in revenue, nice business. I'll put a team together after the meeting. Other than that, [shuffles papers] let's keep the ball in the fairway and out of the hazards."

Escher popped his head up, leaned back into his plush leather high-backed chair and interlaced his fingers behind his head. Hearing the detailed reports of his employees' labor had an almost erotic effect on him.

Fredericks scrolled through his phone. "Bale and I will start the target list for Landy's, pull together a teaser and confidentiality agreement. We will also finish buyer calls for Tracix Corp."

"Who are the buyers for that?"

"All contract logistics, mid-sized. We've sent C.A.s out to most of them," Fredericks said, referring to a confidentiality agreement.

"OK, OK. Keep me abreast of the situation there. Who's next? Mike?"

McAllister ticked off the projects on his fingers with a stout fountain pen his rancher dad bought for him when he got that first job as a trader.

"Alright, Robert, for this week I got the Fairfax pitch, the Boeing buyside financing memo, I will also be helping Fredericks make calls for Tracix, and work to finish the Billings Inc valuation—"

"*The never-ending* valuation," Robert deadpanned. They all chuckled.

"God, how long have we been on that?"

"Since I started here, at least," McAllister said. "Worst clients I have ever worked with."

Of course it is awful, it's an Escher project, Bale

thought, surreptitiously studying the man who, he now noticed, was wearing a black suit jacket with navy trousers, a faux pas he was sure McAllister would ridicule later.

He thought about Escher, his hair like a chunk of cigar ash, his belly like a sack of pennies sagging over his belt buckle. He started the firm with Goldman fifteen years ago with his wife's family money and connections. Before, he had slowly climbed the ranks at traditional banks in various actuarial roles.

Gum-chomping Goldman, conversely, rose up through the ranks, analyst through vice president, at Credit Suisse in New York. They asked him to start the Chicago branch. Goldman was someone junior bankers would naturally strive—kill each other—to be, with his country club scratch golf, board appointments, newspaper-profiled wine cellar, yacht and blood-red Porsche. Occasionally, the "Chic*awgo*" of his son-of-a-janitor childhood shined through. This made Goldman mythical.

Goldman and the other senior bankers had the intellectual horsepower for finance but worked hardest at smooth pitch-making and winning new clients, the means to ever-more cash. Escher had it backwards. Professorial and frumpy, he could tell you the sine of 45 degrees without a calculator and loved restructuring and valuation work—the people-free, mathematical, orbiting satellites of the investment banking solar system.

Escher types make great junior bankers, able to grind through endless Excel and PowerPoint drudgery, but they rarely make it to managing director. The fact that he was a managing partner exposed, for Bale, some ghastly malfunction in the carefully ordered capitalist system that people—like his own father—demanded be trusted and revered.

Escher didn't grin at you the way Fredericks or McAllister or even Goldman did—all knowing the work they were assigning was excruciating but necessary. That the competitive rush of hardcore deal-making and its six-zero payouts was motivation enough to pry one's way into this business and to step without concern over the bleeding bodies of your quote-unquote colleagues.

"This career is your straightest path to making millions of dollars in the shortest time possible," he remembered his father, Bruce, telling him as he neared graduation, in his latest lecture on personal responsibility. "Having 'fuck you' money."

Bale remembered his father had a fierce competitiveness in him that would have put the bankers to shame. It wasn't quite sociopathy, but it was unquenchable.

In his pre-fatherhood days, Bruce's attitude came off as confidence rather than misanthropy. At least that's how Ruth judged it when they met at a mutual friend's birthday the first summer after college. By the time Bale was old enough to *really* know him, Bruce was treating even a common business meeting as a zero-sum game, transformed as he aged by an obsession with his own hastening mortality. Outside of work, he'd smash a golf club into a tree trunk if he lost a bet to an old friend.

"Thanks for the update, McAllister," Goldman said. He looked up from his printed emails. "Who's next? Bale?"

"Yes. I am doing the teaser and C.A. for Landy's, making prospective buyer calls for Tracix, and developing marketing materials for PCP, DT Aerospace, and Revé Nous."

"OK, sounds good," Goldman said. "Mr. Rothkauf, what do you have?"

"Cleaver management presentation, the Dyer Casting pitch, and the Boeing memo," Rothkauf said. "Also, a reminder that I will be on vacation next week."

"Um, *OK*," Goldman said, his leg twitching under the table. This was always a terrible sign. "Does anyone have anything else?"

Jim Cross suddenly tore into the conference room carrying a garment bag draped over his shoulder. For essentially this reason they called him "The Hurricane."

"Sorry I am late, boys—back in town from the SR closing dinner."

"How'd it go?" Goldman said.

"Schmoozing and boozing," he said as he plopped himself into an open chair. "So, we're finishing up dinner and the waiter drops off the check and Dennis starts stuttering and looking at me and I had to gently remind him, with the entire table locked on us, that not only was he contractually obligated to pay for the closing dinner but also that he could just take it out of the *$85 million dollars in cash* I just handed him."

They chuckled.

"I have nothing to report on that front other than Dennis praising our efforts. They love us. He mentioned he would connect me with a friend of his who runs an asbestos abatement contracting company that he wants to sell. Mesothelioma lawsuits are stacking up. No financial data yet. I am scheduling a meeting with them for next week in Tampa."

Cross was truly a unique specimen in the investment banking world. At 36, he was probably the youngest managing director at a major firm. Apart from his energy and commitment to hunting and fishing, he was also one of the only managing directors, or M.D.s, as they were known, who rose from an entry-level analyst job to the top brass at a single firm. It's just too miserable a path. Enemies are made too easily.

Cross joined Goldman & Coli when the place was just two phone lines and a University of Chicago M.B.A. candidate who spoke almost no English and was happy to get paid $100/day to tackle behind-the-scenes grunt work. After an entire summer of awkward, sign language-type interactions, G&C decided that they should bite the bullet and spring for a proper analyst.

It wasn't that Escher failed to attend a University of Chicago "super Saturday" career fest, interviewing geeky finance and accounting majors. He had gone. But he forgot to check his appearance in the mirror and conducted ten half-hour interviews with a lunchtime BBQ stain on his cheek. Three offers extended; none accepted.

While Escher was doing this, his partner Robert Goldman was at Augusta National Golf Club playing, quite frankly, the fucking round of his life.

He nailed a birdie on #16 and was shooting par, on track to possibly break his all-time best of -1, when on #17 he landed in a soggy sand trap past a set of trees on a dogleg right, some eighty yards from the hole.

He vocalized his strategy and demanded a sand wedge to his equally tan and sweating but scrawny and skeptical caddy, who was viewing the pin's location through cupped hands.

That caddy was Jim "the Hurricane" Cross, then a physics major who gave Goldman a Georgia-accented earful on spherical permutational resistance in deep humidity and probability outcomes, and refused Goldman his wedge.

Goldman, visibly irritated, was about to threaten the kid's job when Cross snuggled up behind him, forced a six iron into his hands, and demonstrated the *exact* swing Goldman should make.

Cross stepped out of sight. The story goes that Goldman's shot leapt off the club face, threading two trees, spun clockwise like "the wheels on mah Thunderbird" Cross yelled afterward, and died dramatically after two big bounces through the ruff, rolling into the hole with a soft kerplunk.

Goldman, usually a regal human being, could be seen from the club house riding his six iron around the fairway like a colt, screaming and smacking the phantom's hide, while Cross "yee-hawed" him on.

Cross was hired that day.

"Good work, Jim. Thanks," Goldman said, chomping his gum mercilessly. "We're good for the week."

Shuffling papers. Physical adjustments.

"I do want to say," Goldman added, "that if we continue at this pace and everything closes on time, we will post our biggest year in firm history. So, let's keep up the work."

The group lifted themselves from the high-backed office chairs. There was some small, meaningless chatter, in between which Escher crammed the rest of his bagel into his quivering lips, which ended up wearing a crescent of dried cream cheese for much of the morning.

Goldman pushed the conference button: "Sher? Sher?"

"Yes, Robert?"

"We're done in here. Thanks."

9:30 a.m.

They filed out back to their desks. Goldman and Coli and The Hurricane passed to their offices and after their office doors slammed the analysts and associates met in the center of the bullpen as Sherry walked through, en route to tidying up.

"Dude, you're an investment banker," McAllister said to Rothkauf. "Will you get some fucking proper slacks?"

"Ha ha ha."

"You look like shit, dude."

"Rothkauf's a little golfer," Fredericks said. "A little vacation in the works, there, Jaybers? Goldman didn't seem too happy."

"Ha ha, no, he's fine," Rothkauf said. "Danny and I are going on our annual trip to Scotland. Just a week with a weekend on either side."

"Well that *will* be enjoyable. And why do you say 'Danny' like any of us know who the fuck that is? And your Friday night, McAllister?"

"Stephanie and I met some of her sorority friends at Halligan."

"Uh oh," Bale said.

"Yeah, things aren't the best there. Been fighting a lot. Mainly about the lack of time we spend together and—"

"Everything OK?" Bale said.

"She told me over the weekend it was obvious I don't *truly* love her. Though I am not sure how she could possibly know my innermost thoughts. How about you, Bale?"

"Took my mom for ribs at Twin Anchors to celebrate her birthday. Drinks with high school buds afterward."

"Reasonable," Fredericks said. "But you can't beat my weekend. I got home Friday at 4:30 in the morning after having ten drinks and my wife had me up at 9:30 to take the cats to their spa. Then I went to the eco-friendly dry cleaners, Lowes for a new vacuum cleaner, and then spent three hours cleaning the house which was crucial because" [he already had begun laughing and throat snorting and waving his hand] *because* I had to get it ready for the *team* of people that I pay $300 to clean my house."

"Terrible," McAllister said as he scrolled through emails. "Absolutely terrible."

"But Saturday night was enjoyable," Fredericks said, "I ordered a deep-dish pizza—the one with an inch of fake cheese and a sausage wheel—and ate it in bed while drinking a bottle of red wine and passed out at 9. I woke up with the cat licking my face."

"Sunday was brutal for me," McAllister interjected. "Six and half hours on the Tracix deal."

"Yeah," Fredericks said, "I was sitting right *there* [pointed to his cubicle] keying data."

"Christ," Bale said. "You could've sent some my way—or done the entry from home."

"Naw, daddy needs the *desktop* to key his data," Fredericks said. "Ergonomics, baby. That ain't new. And plus," he added, "I was here from 9:30 a.m. until 3:30— and you weren't."

"Got here at 4."

"And you had to stay all night, I bet."

"Would've had to either way. Escher changed so many things in the pitch that I would've had to keep coming *back*."

"Working with that guy every day is like teaching a 16-year-old girl how to give a blowjob," Fredericks said.

The others roared. Bale winced.

"Whooooa man, that's terrible," Bale said.

Fredericks' eyes locked on Bale's, but it was McAllister who intervened.

"It's a fucking *joke* man," McAllister said. "You better learn to laugh if you want to survive in his industry."

McAllister quickly pivoted to Rothkauf. "Nice shirt, Rothy. You wore it Thursday."

"Good attention to detail."

"I didn't like it last week and I don't like it this week," McAllister added.

"I didn't like *you* last week and you're still here," J. B. said.

McAllister play-lunged at him.

An office door opened and slammed in the main corridor. The bullpenners hurried back to their desks.

10 a.m.

For a time, you could hear the clicking and typing of keys, the shuffling of documents under review, and pitch calls.

Ballon walked to Fredericks' cube to ask him to explain the discount rate Escher demanded for his DCF, but Fredericks was on the phone. Fredericks turned and gave Bale an exaggerated gesture to his phone to indicate his busy annoyance.

"Jack, you may want to put your fork down," Fredericks said into the phone. "Tell me, do you like money and pussy? Cause I've got a little of both for ya."

. . . . .

By July, his second month at the firm, Bale's mother-board had been re-wired to life at Goldman & Coli, LLC. All he had to do was keep going.

The iPhone alarm rang at—

6:45 a.m.

—he smacked it.

He got up, walked to the kitchen to make coffee, and turned on CNBC. The cackling analysts filled the living room.

Every few minutes his phone vibrated. Every time it did this he paused, waiting to hear a repeat vibration, signaling a possible phone call from one of the partners, instead of an email or text. He doted on his phone like an infant.

While slurping his second of usually six daily coffees, he walked to the bay windows and stood near the ajar glass and breathed the sugary lake breeze.

Out his window, he looked at the quivering orb rising over the lakefront. He watched a little white boat sailing outward in the direction of his family's lake house.

He suddenly remembered running up the bluff below the house, his knee swollen from a bee sting when he was perhaps three or four. It was his earliest memory, seeing the tight coils of his mother's dangling black hair and round flushed cheeks as she rushed him into her arms. His father was fucking around with some machine in the tool shed, yelling to her to bring him something Bale couldn't make out. He emptied his eyes, face pressed into her arms, his eyes staring at the pink flesh swelling around his dangling knee cap.

"All pain is temporary," she told him, sweeping strands of his sweaty hair behind his ears with her nails.

It was the women in his family who were the people of substance. His grandmother was a librarian at University of Chicago for thirty years, while Ruth was a book editor at a downtown publishing house when she struck up a conversation with Bruce at that friend's party.

After they wed, having vanquished the male competition, Bruce threw virtually all of himself into his business. It was a forced conclusion rather than a choice for Ruth to leave book editing at that point to raise Bale. Even so, their marriage never withered so much as stunted, a credit to his mother's compassion and love. She devoted herself to motherhood, the occasional freelance book editing project and a string of philanthropic board positions as the years went on and Bruce's business soared. She also occupied her fiery mind with meditative conquests like gardening and *New York Times* crosswords, tempered by a single nightly cabernet sauvignon.

Even a few months before he started at Goldman, Bale could sense Ruth again pushing aside her bibliophilia to align with his father's demands.

Thinking about his father's demands reminded Bale of Meta, his first love torn from him in sickening fashion at just the infancy of their relationship. Had it really been a *year* since they were leaning into each other that last night on a foot bridge over the River Thames, his lips pressed to her forehead that somehow always smelled like summer.

Now in July, separated by hundreds of miles, her scent tortured him on the breeze. Thinking about her now was like waking from a beautiful dream into the stagnant purgatory of his new life. He battled the rising feelings of guilt and sadness and disconnectedness.

Had he made the right choice? Had he destroyed his only chance at happiness?

A cab's screeching brakes drew his attention back to the morning routine.

Fredericks, describing his routine, had once said: "In the morning I turn the shower on and lay naked in my tub like a beached whale."

Bale showered. Sometimes his eyes were red and swollen from a lack of sleep. The scalding water usually helped.

Next, he was required to dress very well. He slid into charcoal Hugo Boss slacks and a pin-dot Canali shirt.

Next, Goldman neurotically required that his employees shave their faces daily.

Bale took his laptop and work bag, locked the

door, and walked down the corridor to the elevator.

And, like all investment bankers do for more than half their lives, Bale moved from one sterile, temperature-controlled enclosure to another, his living and working spaces separate but no longer different.

12:12 p.m.

When Bale got back to his desk, his laptop was missing.

He went around the cubicle to Fredericks' desk, festooned with Iowa Hawkeyes paraphernalia.

"Hey man, did you take my computer?"

"Take *what*?"

"It's gone; did you take it?"

"Your *computer*?" Fredericks said. "No." He laughed. "Takes a lot of skill to lose a computer in an office. Good work, son."

He went to McAllister's desk and found him craned over his monitor scanning photos his dad sent him from a recent Calgary cattle auction.

"Give it back, McAllister. I got a lot on my plate."

Without turning, McAllister said: "Give what back? Hey, do you know anything about butterfly spreads?"

"I studied them, but no. Come on, man."

"You're not an expert in anything, B. R. That is a major problem."

"Give it back, man. I got a lot before lunch."

"Lunch! Great point."

"Where to, McAllister?" Fredericks said.

"Chipotle."

"That place is a toilet."

"It's so tasty."

"I'll be sick all day."

"Get one of those salad-type things."

Fredericks jiggled his belly.

"Bale, you in?"

"Not going anywhere until I get my fucking computer back," he said, scanning along the cubicle's undercarriage. "Such a waste of time."

"Ease up, dude," McAllister said. "Maybe you put it in the same drawer you kept that wrinkled shirt you're wearing."

"This shirt just came back from the dry cleaners," Bale said, checking Fredericks' trash can and then moving to his file cabinet.

"Then why are there two long lines running down the front of it?" McAllister said. He and Fredericks had moved and were euphoric watching him rummage around the cubicle.

"They fold it with cardboard and plastic," Bale said, "for traveling purposes."

"Traveling?" McAllister said, running his hands through his gelled coal-black hair. Tell them to put it on a fucking hanger so you don't look like a pile of shit at work. This isn't the trading floor at the fucking Merc, it's an investment bank."

"Where is my computer?"

"If you help convince Fredericks that Chipotle is viable," McAllister said, "I might decide to help you look for it."

"Fredericks," Bale said, arm deep in Fredericks' file cabinet and squinting and gasping, "you have an *amazing* body. Chipotle won't change that."

"When you get to my age, it's not about looking good anymore," Fredericks said, "it's about not dying."

Bale looked at McAllister. "Come on, man."

McAllister ignored him. He called out to Fredericks: "Hey, do you know anything about butterfly spreads?"

"Ask Rothkauf—that's the move he used last Saturday night with *Danny*."

"Ha ha ha," rang out from Rothkauf's cube.

"Do you know who took my computer, Jaybers?"

"McAllister hid it by his trash can."

"*You asshole!*" McAllister yelled.

Bale bent down and removed his computer and took it back to his cubicle and docked it. He noticed they had yanked out all of the cords to the docking station as well as those connected to his double-paneled power strip.

"Goddamn it, Rothkauf. I wanted to see him get really flustered."

They watched Bale crawling around under the desk futzing with the wires.

"You ready, little guy?" Fredericks pressed. "A little lunch?"

"One minute. One minute."

Rothkauf came to the entrance of the cubicle. The three of them watched Bale.

"How about we go to the Union League Club?" J. B. said, "They have a great buffet."

"Lunch buffets are for nursing homes," Fredericks said.

"How long, little guy?"

"I have to reboot, and I have to send one email. Then we can go."

There was no response from the three. They just watched him on his knees, fiddling with the tangled labyrinth of chords and plugs.

"You guys wanna hold the little twerp down while I rape him?" Fredericks said.

1:52 p.m.

Standing inside his cubicle, buzzed and bloated with the sour caloric taste of onions and salt and guacamole, Ballon was tabulating his to-the-minute caffeine intake, counting aloud and on his fingers.

He was just about to go chug a bucket of ice water when Escher entered his cubicle.

Escher had a piece of toilet paper stuck to his shoe.

"Bale, can you compile a list of domestic companies in the aerospace industry, revenues between $50 million and $200 million? Include the name, revenues, descriptions, and relevant contacts. You may have to call them to tease out the info." But then Escher added, in his pseudo-apologetic manner, that he did not like the Capital IQ company descriptions—that is, the descriptions that are pre-written in the subscription database. He wanted Ballon to write them from scratch, "by visiting the company's website and reading articles and press releases."

Jesus fucking Christ.

"When do you think I can have it? I mean, I am going out of town tomorrow morning at 11 a.m. and it would be great to look at something tonight, if you can."

"I have some research to do for Jim and I also have to put together some slides on the middle-market conditions of buy-side transactions. He wants that by tomorrow, too."

Bale left a little pause as an opportunity for Escher to ease up on the deadline, which he, of course, did not.

Escher tapped the walls of Ballon's cubicle and left.

He used his little sugar and caffeine high to his advantage. He opened Capital IQ and defined the search parameters and set about formatting the results.

Bale mouthed his malcontent: *This dog shit fucking work. I got fifteen fucking tasks to complete. Don't we have a fucking intern?*

Fredericks appeared in the cubicle, eating an apple, munching as Ballon pounded the keys. He could feel Fredericks' pleasure as he watched. Something like,

"You see, little guy, I was sitting where you were, but I made it to the next level. Now you do the bullshit."

"Hey there, puke sack."

Ballon laughed without turning.

"How long do you think it would take someone to notice if you died?" Fredericks said.

"Like if I disappeared in person or like, electronically?" Bale said, his keyboarding like thunder.

"In person. If you died right now, in your chair, inside your cubicle at work, when would someone notice?"

Ballon stopped and swiveled to face him.

"Fuck," he said.

"Really hit you in the mind with that one, didn't I?" Fredericks said, chewing apple.

"Well, since Escher has come by my fucking desk twelve times bringing me heaps of work I would say roughly 28 minutes."

"Shit, yeah!" Fredericks said, aping his grandad's Iowa trailer park drawl.

"Escher just handed me a de-pinned grenade."

"Uh huh." Munching munching munching.

"That guy can be a sack of cunt gravy," Fredericks said.

Bale wheeze-laughed.

"I got 700 things to do for Goldman, but he wants this by tonight. It's not even a real deadline."

"You need some help?" Fredericks said.

Bale paused considering how rare it was to hear

an associate ask that question to an analyst.

"Thank you, but no. I just need to keep moving on this."

"Cool. Let me know," Fredericks said. "Anyway, I am right there with you. I'll be here till midnight working on Sherry's financial model—"

"They have her doing analyst work?"

"They should leave the ape work to the apes, right? I mean, they don't ask me to put heels on and look hot, do they?"

"No, they don't."

Bale turned back to his keyboard. He decided to say it: "Is Sherry getting paid for analyst-level work? I thought she just did admin stuff?

"What do you mean?" he said, grinning.

"I mean, she is doing the same level of work as me but for a lot less money?"

Fredericks got serious. "Careful—you don't want to tell your bosses that you think you are being *overpaid*."

"Right but—"

"Everyone here is slammed with work, we were just asking her to help a little. I mean, do you want more work to do? You're still running through the jungle at least. McAllister's got a fork in him and is being turned over the fire."

"That bad?"

"Pitch Friday. Pitch Monday," Fredericks said.

"Jesus."

"Yep."

"Hmmm, weekend completely destroyed by work because of a Monday pitch. Lemme guess. Hurricane?" Bale said, referring to the managing director Jim Cross, the Southern-born ex-caddy who impressed Goldman on the golf course those many years ago.

"Every time."

"Every fucking time."

"Well, I'll let you get to it."

"Any advice for me?" Bale said.

"Yep. If you don't eat it, you *are* it."

"Thanks."

"And if you eat it wrong, you're basically eating dong."

Bale's laugh quickly faded into disgust and then apathy as he found his rhythm again and became lost in the sequence of muscle memory. Later, he paused and massaged his eyes. His high was fading, and he thought ahead to another fifteen-hour workday.

6:15 p.m.

The office was filled by the static whirl of the machines, breathing, pulsating, blinking. The Prius-sized printer eee-ed and aww-ed as it tattooed paper.

Ballon and McAllister were in Goldman's office discussing DT Aerospace, going over changes before the management presentation. They had only found two buyers.

"One lacks synergies," Goldman said, "and the

other buried millions in the earnout—Bale, that means an incentive for the existing management to stay with the company after it's sold. The average age of the management team is 76. We're lucky if these guys don't fucking die before we close the deal."

7:15 p.m.

Escher came back to Ballon's desk.

"Hi there. How's it going?"

"Just fine. You?"

"Good. Good. Listen, I have an appointment. I'll be back in a couple of hours to check on the work."

He walked off.

7:35 p.m.

The senior bankers had all gone home.

"What font do you want this in, McAllister?" Bale said.

McAllister shrieked in a girlish Indian accent: "GARI-MOND!"

It sparked Fredericks' taste buds. "Papa needs some vindaloo. J.B., it's your turn to order. J. B.?"

"Don't think he's here," McAllister said, spinning around to check. "Nope."

"God, where *is* that guy," Fredericks said, getting up and going over to his cubicle.

"I'll order it," Bale said. "Menu's in my drawer."

McAllister came over and snatched and scanned.

A minute later, Fredericks burst into laughter from J. B.'s cubicle and then came into Bale's.

"Check your email," Fredericks said.

Ballon opened his email:

"I like to play with myself and then tuck it in between my legs and pretend I'm a woman!!!! XOXO, J. B."

"Who did you send it to?" Ballon said.

"Bullpen plus Hurricane," Fredericks said. "He loves that shit."

"Fredericks. Dinner. Choose," McAllister said handing him the menu.

"Don't need to look. Chicken vindaloo," Fredericks said. "But you'll probably go with some weak shit like *tikka*."

McAllister considered, scanning the menu. "Cream-based curry is probably the worst thing in the world for you—thousands of calories and fat," McAllister said.

"Youuu puussy," Fredericks said.

"I *am* going with chicken tikka. This place does it well. Charcoaled. Light."

"Same," Ballon said.

"Nonsense," Fredericks said. "If you had two testicles you'd go with the murg makhani instead of the tikka like some anorexic sorority whore."

"And get one of those for Jaybers, too," Martin

added. "Wouldn't want to see the little guy go hungry."

"Hey, guys," J. B. said, standing behind Fredericks.

"Holy shit, J. B., you scared me. Where the hell were you?"

"In the bathroom. Is that alright?"

"Not when we are ordering. We put you down for a little dish called murg makhani."

"Sounds good. Naan, too."

"Naan! Don't you worry yourself little fella," Fredericks said. "We'll do three orders of garlic naan and various chutneys."

Fredericks picked up the menu and handed it to J. B.

"Order well. Client is paying."

Martin went to his cubicle and retrieved a small football. McAllister and Bale stood at opposite sides of the bullpen and tossed it back and forth.

McAllister's phone rang and he ran back to his desk. Fredericks instructed Ballon to run buttonhooks down the long corridor that led to the lobby. He made a great show of throwing tight spirals into Bale's heaving chest.

8:35 p.m.

Trays were spread across the conference room table.

"Look at us, like animals," J. B. said stuffing naan into his mouth.

"Wealthy, good-looking animals," McAllister said with his mouth full.

"How's the murg, Jaybers?" Fredericks said.

"Money."

"You know papa's got your back. That ain't new."

"You know what would be really nice?" J. B. said, knowing how absurd his coming suggestion was. "If after this nice, leisurely dinner, we could all just leave and go to Stocks and Blondes and have a beer. Nothing crazy. Just a relaxing gathering of gentlemen."

There was a silence while they all dreamed of it. Walking together, laughing, sitting in the crowded hole under the "El" tracks. Watching the strung-out traders in their vests yammer at women hugging the bar.

"Love to, but I've got 18 inches of horse dick in my bag tonight," Fredericks said, spearing a piece of chicken from his aluminum tray. "Remember gentlemen, when you're a banker, misery equals money."

"The two are positively correlated," McAllister said.

"But we are also promoting efficiency in the marketplace, helping entrepreneurs cash in on their life's work," Bale said.

Fredericks' mouth fell open. McAllister spit rice across the table he laughed so hard.

"Dude. *What the fuck are you talking about*?" McAllister said.

"Other motivations," Bale said, his face reddened.

"I just want to make a fuckton of money," Fredericks said.

"Same," McAllister said.

"He's right though," Rothkauf said. "You gotta have something else motivating you in life besides money."

"Says the guy with a massive trust fund," McAllister said.

"Oh shit, Escher will be back any minute," Bale said. "Haven't finished his work."

"You better get moving son," Fredericks said. "Take your tray to your desk."

"I mean, I was powering through it all day, just got backlogged. Don't you think he'll underst—?

"No," they all said in unison.

"Alright. *Fine*," Ballon said, shoveling a saucy forkful of rice-speckled curry into his mouth, "I fucking hate that guy."

9:42 p.m.

Back at his desk, Bale found his rhythm again and soon he was so deep into the work he didn't notice the time. It took McAllister kicking the back of his chair to bring him back.

"Christ, you scared the shit out of me."

"You're too high-strung, dude. Gotta be chill like me."

Fredericks had his computer bag over his shoulder.

"Getting' outta this bitch. Gotta catch the 10:15," he said, walking off.

"You need me to do anything tonight?"

"Eat a bum's ass and get a piss shower, you homo," Fredericks said, walking off.

Bale closed his eyes and sighed. He realized his hands were shaking and rubbed them together. He tried to block out Fredericks' hate and sat in silence for a few minutes trying to will himself out of a demoralized funk.

He heard the faint hum of the refrigerator in the kitchen and the donkey-like sounds of the printer, and, in the distance, the roar of an ambulance speeding through downtown.

"Rothy? You there," he called out.

"Still here man. Still here."

Ballon got up and walked to his desk.

"Escher ditched me here. Worked all day on his fucking list. He said he needed to review it tonight. Nope. Nothing. Now I have at least five hours of other work to do, the stuff I was supposed to be doing all day."

Rothkauf cleared his throat as an indication of his sympathy and nodded in agreement.

"What you got going?"

"The Hurricane has me writing a business plan for a biomedical start-up.

"Interesting.

"Hurricane hopes it'll position us to do their IPO in five years."

"When's it due back to him?"

"Oh, not for a few days but I know tomorrow is going to be awful."

"Really? Why?"

"Because every day is."

10:42 p.m.

He scrolled down his Excel list for Escher. He had forty-two companies. Names, originally written company descriptions, name of a "key" company official, and contact information. He even embedded website links into the company logos.

His professional aptitude depended to an astonishing degree on correct formatting.

He checked his email. Something from Fredericks:

"Hey there pukebag—Just got an email from Hurricane. He is in Dallas. Can you overnight him a printout of the QRL pitch? Version 8. Should be in my recent documents. He is leaving the hotel at 3 p.m. for his plane home. Wants to review it then. He is staying at the Sheraton in Dallas. Call the desk and tell them you are sending it. Thanks bud."

He went to Fredericks' cube. He edited, printed, and bound the presentation and then checked it page by page for errors. He then went through it three more times.

He thought about Brad Katzman, his JPMorgan friend he met during his semester abroad in London. Katzman, a grunting stocky misanthrope with impeccable cleanliness and disdain for humanity, was the prototypical country club Republican, materialistic and ingeniously shallow. Not a hair follicle askew, a glossy poof over Prada glasses and a jawless sneering face. A single-issue voter. A zero-sum genius. The type of man who trained hidden cameras on the help, who added a wife and pug to his life for the image it creates in the minds of others.

He thought about Katzman at his desk at JPMorgan, where he'd interned two summers in a row before graduation, working a nauseating hundred hours a week, while Ballon averaged eighty-five. Brad made more money, but his New York City rent was much higher, and his associate treated him like a farm hand shit shoveler. Fredericks was money, apart from his brutal insults and misogyny.

Bale printed a FedEx label and put it on the envelope. He would drop it off on his way home.

1:55 a.m.

Ballon was bleary and fading. His head pulsed. His neck gyrated. His hands shook as his fingers drummed the keyboard. He battled exhaustion with the thumping electronica in his ears and fought the buttery caloric monolith in his stomach with caffeine and rage.

He dropped his highlighter and ignored it. He took a fresh one from a mesh-metal cylinder on his desk. His eyes had the wiry alertness of a cocaine addict. He touched his face, felt follicle stubbles over a greasy film. He needed a break but there was nowhere to go and nothing else to do.

He thought of his productivity curve: *in a production system with fixed and variable inputs beyond some point, each additional unit of variable input yields less and less output.*

His work was too slow now.

He had crossed the threshold.

He became angry he *had* a threshold.

He could make it up in the morning, provided Goldman didn't want to see the comps, financials, and industry slides until roughly 11 a.m. He could get in early, finish them by 10 and have McAllister review the work.

He had learned *never* to hand something to a senior banker until it has been reviewed by someone below.

He went to hit ctrl+1 to quickly format some cells but hit the F1 key instead, calling up a *fucking useless* Excel help sidebar.

Escher was a human pop-up window.

He looked at his keyboard and resisted the urge to smash it to pieces on the wood paneling of his cube.

He studied the keys, weighing the importance of each against the utility he derived from each key based on the frequency of usage and time saved.

He took a mechanical pencil from the mesh-metal bin and with its tip he pried the F1 key from its root until it popped off and flew to the back of his cubicle. He smiled. He studied the keys. He attacked the function keys, prying them and popping them like corn kernels in a hot kettle. His smile widened. Then he pried up the Caps Lock key, which arced and fell into his trashcan.

Swoosh!

He then yanked his mouse out of the back of the dock and chucked it against the wall. The thud and shatter of the plastic parts was loud and perverse against the silence of the office.

The mouse lay in pieces under a machine-made painting. There was a little gray stripe where plastic hit paint, a little indelible mark.

He giggled.

He grew wild, restless:

"Where *is* Escher?" he said to his computer screen. Then he screamed: "Where the fuck is Escher?!"

It didn't matter; there was no one left in the building but the security guards sitting in the lobby. The cleaning staff was long gone. He was alone.

If an analyst screams in an empty office building, does he produce a sound?

Now, Fredericks, Bale thought, I can drop dead and no one would know until the morning.

2:30 a.m.

Bale exited the elevators into the glass lobby of the Willis Tower. He walked slowly, wearily. He felt haggard and dirty. He was sweating from his armpits. The tops of his feet itched hellishly under his Ferragamo shoes, picked out by McAllister, who joked that his father's cowboys would hang him from a tree if he showed up on the Alberta ranch in such a glossy pair.

Bale's fingers shook as they lifted a Parliament from its pack.

He hailed a cab and climbed in.

The driver took him down Wacker Drive, the little sallow lights blurred against the city's darkness.

He sucked in a very fine drag of smoke, exhaling in a tight cylinder that was vacuumed out the cracked window and lifted high up into the moon-chilled air. The thought of ascension reminded him of the aspirations he had for his FedEx package, sitting next to his quivering leg.

As they drove, he heard the grinding rattling obsolete weight of the "El" train at Lake Street, and then saw the buildings high over the Chicago River. He saw a homeless man and his child cross the street against the light. His cab driver honked at them and then swerved. The child flinched; his father did not. The cab driver was speaking eloquent French into a headset.

As they were approaching Wacker and Clark, Bale said: "Stop here and wait."

The man pulled over and Bale exited, leaving the door open. He flicked his cigarette and marched into the 24-hour FedEx outpost.

The fluorescent lights were sharp. Bale could tell the employee was startled by his red eyes balanced over mush-gray bags.

"Send this package overnight to Dallas. Here is

the address. Will it get there by 2 p.m.?"

"One p.m., sir."

"Fine. Thank you."

As he saw the brilliant lights of Michigan Avenue glow in the weird atmosphere, he suddenly remembered a family lunch at the café at the Ritz off of Michigan Avenue after he graduated from high school and his father's life-long friend Blake Schepp standing to give a toast. Schepp, a managing partner at Credit Suisse, had arranged for Bale's paper-pushing summer internship at a hedge fund and, later, for that job interview with Escher, who had been Schepp's roommate in college.

"Bale, you continue to impress us all," Schepp said, pinching the stem of his Syrah, lifted toward the 18-year-old.

"We all have to find our own purpose in life. Wherever you go, whatever you strive to accomplish, know that we expect much from you but will always be there to support you. Congratulations."

The family applauded tastefully. Schepp then reached into the inside pocket of his dark suit and pulled out a rectangular card, which he pressed into Bale's palm. Bale thanked him, they shook hands firmly, and the group sipped from their drinks.

After a few minutes, Ballon excused himself and meandered to the edge of the restaurant to read his card. Opening the envelope, he found a stock certificate for a $500-stake in a blue-chip company and a folded piece of paper that opened to Kipling's *If*.

His eyes were drawn most to the last lines, and he read them twice.

If you can fill the unforgiving minute
With sixty seconds' worth of distance run,
Yours is the Earth and everything that's in it,
And—which is more—you'll be a Man, my son!

When he walked back into the dining area, through the islands of relatives fingering blueberry muffins and sipping coffee from tiny cups, he saw outside the glimmering Willis Tower rising above the other buildings, its antennae stabbing the azure sky, and its windows reflecting the waning afternoon sun.

He had imagined soaring miles above the masses, as if that was the best thing a man could do.

He arrived at his apartment, filled with unoriginal products from expensive national chain stores with good return policies.

There was a ladder-like shelving system sprinkled with books, wood trays atop leather ottomans flanked by a leather couch and matching chair. Of the five surfaces available for artwork on the apartment's greywashed walls, one was filled with a massive mirror and the others shared the staggered distribution of four black and white photographs of famous American buildings.

He walked through the bedroom to the closet and removed his clothing, hung his pants, placed his shoes in the metal shoe rack and inserted the wooden shape holders.

As he was plugging in his iPhone next to his bed he saw a text from Meta.

[3:35 AM] Meta Hadley: you awake?

[3:36 AM] Ballon Ratcliffe: Yah just getting home from work. how are you?

[3:36 AM] Meta Hadley: That's brutal! I'm great. Dress rehearsals started this week—going well but exhausted.

[3:37 AM] Ballon Ratcliffe: That's wonderful on rehearsals. So happy for you.

[3:37 AM] Meta Hadley: You know I despise small talk. I miss you. I miss London. I miss what we had.

Bale thought about how to respond but every natural response that bubbled up in his mind seemed like an unfair dead end. They had these stunted, brutal exchanges periodically since they returned to the U.S. from the semester abroad, wanting desperately to preserve some sort of baseline friendship and connection, feebly trying to fend off severing ties completely.

[3:38 AM] Ballon Ratcliffe: Me too.

[3:38 AM] Meta Hadley: Then come to New York. Fuck your miserable job and fuck your dad. Or I'll come to Chicago.

[3:38 AM] Ballon Ratcliffe: I couldn't ask you to do that. It would fuck up your theater work. Wouldn't be right.

[3:39 AM] Meta Hadley: What do you know about what's 'right?'

[3:39 AM] Ballon Ratcliffe: Ouch.

[3:40 AM] Meta Hadley: I give up.

He thought about how exciting their life together had been for those fleeting months in London. Her staggering eyes and form and intelligence. How superhuman or soothed he felt in her arms.

It was absurd that he couldn't now picture her, that he knew only the vague outlines of her New York City life, when London—their fiery and revelatory submersion into body-entangling love—was just a few months ago.

He hung his head, the phone gripped in his sweaty fingertips, and started sobbing.

INTERLUDE LONDON

January–February 2018

Early January. They collided badly. Literally crossed paths, compressed their bodies into each other and expelled air, totings. They buckled with surprise.

Bale—wearing faded jeans, a quarter-zip sweater, and white Converses—clutched three volumes of poetry, a notepad, pen, and a school lounge coffee as he trotted down the stairs of the main university building between classes, to have a sandwich.

Meta—in jeans, carrying a massive taupe Longchamp bag and also caffeine—was rapid-fire speaking by mobile to her agent in New York about a role he was urging her to take.

Their coffees volcanoed on contact. Covered the sidewalk. Doused Bale's beloved literary materials, Meta's mobile phone. The other items scattered comically.

They quickly crouched down to scoop up their items, prevent the coffee from saturating everything.

Their faces drew close together.

Inches from her face, he stole a glance at her eyes, hazel with swirling rays of rusted green and auburn luster, like a solar system swirling around a black hole. She tucked tendrils of caramel-colored hair behind her coin-shaped ears, though her shoulders remained swept back confidently straighter than a fence post as she scooped up her things.

"I am so sorry," Bale said.

"It's fine, it's fine," she said, "I was talking."

"Hand me my glasses?"

"Less is more," he said, immediately regretting the joke.

She rolled her eyes at him, but also chuckled.

Her upturned palm jetted out.

He handed them over.

He shook coffee off his books.

"I am between classes," he said.

"Right. Me too, on that break."

"What track?"

"Sociology. Tisch stateside. You?"

"Literature. Middlebury."

"British?"

"Yeah."

"Twentieth century?"

"Yeah."

"What will you do with your life? Teach?"

"I'll write the great American novel."

"It's already been written."

He laughed.

"No, really," she said. "It's called *The Great American Novel*."

"Damn."

"Philip Roth."

"Oy."

"Well," she said, "he wrote so many books one is bound to be one you could have written given enough time."

They looked at each other not asexually.

"I haven't seen you around school," he said.

"Maybe if you paid attention to where you were going."

He laughed.

"But you aren't hurt though, seriously?" he said. "That was not how I expected the boy-bumping-into-girl cliché to feel."

"People think clichés are harmless," she said. "No, they do real damage."

. . . . .

Later January 2018. School House. Dr. Duffy, a sluggish, frail pedagogue slothed around the classroom. Ballon was seated near the front.

"These are a collection of poems, Heaney and Larkin, some Hughes," he said. "Please analyze each by next Monday."

Bale flipped through the packet and stopped at

Annus Mirabilis by Philip Larkin. He read:

> *Sexual intercourse began*
> *In nineteen sixty-three*
> *(which was rather late for me) -*
> *Between the end of the Chatterley ban*
> *And the Beatles' first LP.*

Duffy returned to his desk. His hands shook as he sipped from a tiny water glass. His eyes—two black, shriveled, miserable, burnt chestnuts—swiveled across the room. Spears of hair were pasted diagonally over his crown. It seemed done out of habit rather than style—a gesture to a long-gone woman, perhaps.

"And now about your papers. As I expected, three were fine, a number more were mediocre, though most were actually alarmingly terrible. *Weak tea.* The problem I fear is America's educational system, which is really very *easy*, isn't it? But this misery is still a slight improvement from your previous papers, which were among the worst I've read in my thirty years in academia. We need to raise both the quality of your ideas and the quality of your expression of those ideas. It won't be impossible."

Looks of worry were exchanged.

Duffy handed back the papers.

When he got to Bale he said, "See me after class."

Duffy moved on.

The paper itself was scrawled in shaky red pen.

He had even circled some of the words and above them wrote: "BANAL" and "SLOPPY" and "DICTION."

There was no letter grade.

Eventually the bell rang, and the students filed out. Bale took longer than necessary to pack his belongings. He approached Duffy who was underlining parts of what looked to be private papers.

Bale's heart was working very hard in his chest.

"Hello, lad," Duffy said, shuffling his papers about, gesturing to the chair next to his desk. "Thank you for seeing me."

"Of course, sir."

Duffy sat back into his chair.

"How are you finding this class?"

"Honestly sir, it is the most difficult I've had."

Duffy nodded tightly.

"Yours was one of the best papers I've received this year, if not longer."

Bale's eyes flickered with disbelief. Writing for him was instantly an exhilarating internal journey chasing perfection. A happy compulsion. Smacking out the words on the keyboard to perfect and mold and express the *ideas* that bubbled up from that unknowable wellspring of creativity. A battle that left him calmed and centered, like conquering a mountain hike or tricking a large trout to take your fly in a river's pool.

"I have not given out an A- in 8 years — and have *never* given out a straight A — but was very tempted to break my trend regarding the former, in this one case, though I had to deal with several of your problems, such as reckless word choice and being too vague and obvious in your analysis of the Eliot. Most of all, you seem to constantly betray your natural voice."

Bale could not help but smile.

"I have a strong belief that by semester's end you will have broken my first rule, but you must continue to work exceedingly hard and apply yourself."

"Thank you, sir."

"Not at all," Duffy said. He leaned forward took Bale's paper from him and wrote "B+" and handed it back.

He then scraped together some papers on his desk, pounded them into order, and handed them to Bale. "Please, if you wouldn't mind, will you have a close read through this piece I am preparing for the *New Statesmen*? It is due at week's end."

"Of course."

"Thank you."

"Copyediting or content?"

"Both, if you don't mind. 'Just have at it,' as you Americans say."

He put it in his pack.

"And one more thing. That last A- I gave was to a student of mine who is now Arts editor at the *Guardian*. If your work improves, and you would in fact wish me to do so, I will write her about a work-trial position for you."

· · · · ·

February 2018

The restaurant was glimmering. A four-stem candelabra cast milky shadows over the tables and scores of faces.

They—Ballon Ratcliffe, Sutton DiPrenzio, and Brad Katzman—were celebrating Bale's first byline in the *Guardian*, which Bale told Katzman was "a newspaper, an aggregation of interesting happenings printed on material made from trees that people hold in their hands and that does not have an ON/OFF switch."

Sutton removed from his inner jacket pocket a chunk of severely folded newsprint, peeled it open, and read Bale's review aloud:

"Of all the deranged journalist bastards to stain the cobbled alleys of the nation's capital, Johnson's Billy Forthwryte has to be among other things the least *capable*, being constantly snookered by any human with breasts, sent on far-flung assignments he doesn't understand, and stampeded by his grinning editor."

"Well-written," Sutton said, folding it closed.

"Another round?" a waiter said.

"Three scotches," Katzman said. "And menus."

"We are now entering the realm of the irresponsible," Sutton said.

"My father often tells me," Bale said. "'B. R., on the balance sheet of life, you're a liability.'"

Katzman roared.

"That is astonishing, that he would say something like that to you," Sutton said.

Katzman raised his glass: "To never having to depend on anyone."

They polished off the scotches in front of them.

"Tell us another thing Bruce has said," Sutton said.

Bale thought.

"My dad was in the Marines and he told me a great story about boot camp. You know, hot and stinking Quonset hut in San Diego, 0530, men recovering from the clanging garbage can the Drill Instructor core-walloped with a baseball bat to wake them thirty seconds before. Then a voice boomed like a car backfiring: 'Alllll right, ladies, *aaah*-ten-shun!'

"The one drill instructor walked along the row of cadets with his arms clasped behind him and said:

"'Do youuu knowww what today is?!'

"'It's Sunday, drill sergeant,' twenty souls called back in unison.

"'An' whadda we do on Sundays?'

"They yelled variances such as 'Church!' and 'God!' and 'Jesus!'

"'Alright ladies,' the other D.I. yelled, walking down the row of them, using his arm to cut through the air, axing out the following: 'I want all the Protestants over *here*; all the Lutherans over *here*; all the Catholics over *here*...' on down the line until all the men were on the road and vigorously reshuffled and scooted into newly formed lines, straight as corn rows and just as silent.

"The D.I.s converged on my father, encircled

him. The one in the middle started in with screams so loud the burst of air from his mouth seemed to fire his skull backwards: 'God damnit, Ratman! What th' fuck is wrong wit' you? Are you some kind of fuggin' idiot?'

"'No sir—'

"'Don't you wanna honor your lord and savior Jesus H. Christ?'

"'Yes sir, but, well sir, I'm *Jewish*, sir.'

"The middle instructor flinched in disbelief. He yelled: 'Ho-lee shit, Ratman! You are yanking my chain, aren't you?'

"'No, sir. I would not, sir.'

"'You're a Christ Killer, motherfucker?!'

"The D.I. on the outside, whose brimmed hat was nearly stabbing my father's Adam's apple, spoke up just as the D.I. in the middle was finishing his sentence. His eyes looked like they might burst onto the floor. And, voicing some random, misinformed conclusion he held about Jews and their sexual practices, he said:

"'Have you ever had vagina sex with a woman, Ratman?'

"His question was spoken with such honesty that the three D.I.s leaned in slowly eager for the response.

"'Well, yes sir!' my father said strongly.

"'No shit, Ratman!?' The middle one said: 'And how many women have you slept with?'

"'So many, sir, I lost count, sir!'

"My father's delivery was so natural and loud

and believable that the three D.I.'s literally shot looks at each other and then burst out laughing—something that not only hadn't happened since that boot camp training session commenced but also in the history of that particular MCRD. They continued in big wide-gaped hilarity and soon all the recruits were roaring without reserve. Two of the D.I.s plunged their palms onto their knees to support their torsos weakened from the wonderful levity.

"The D.I.s eventually regained their fascist composure and then snapped to. The first D.I. shouted: 'Well, from here on out, Ratcliffe, you'll be a Lutheran. Now get on the road!'"

Brad and Sutton roared.

"But somehow," Bale continued, "somehow the Brigadier General found out and felt it sent a bad message—or at least could potentially lead to a scandal or lawsuit of some sort—and arranged for a rabbi to come to the camp and lead services for all three Jewish boots. Even brought in bagels and lox."

"You're lying," Katzman said.

"No, no, the rabbi told the Brigadier General it says in the Torah that God commanded Moses to adorn boiled dough with cured salmon and creamed cheese."

· · · · ·

February 20, 2018

Ballon sat alone on the small red sofa in the living room of their flat.

He had made up his mind to tell his father. It simply had to be done.

He dialed the mobile.

"Hello, Father," he said, his voice echoing uncomfortably in the sparse flat.

"My long-lost son! *No, Jennifer, not the Maxwell presentation, the pharmacy one...*"

"Is this a good time?" Bale said.

There was a condescending, overly enunciated tone in Bruce's voice when he was working.

"How's London?"

"It's fine, Dad."

"And your classes? Yes, *Jennifer, the Jenkins Pharmacy file.*"

"British Literature is going very well."

"Good ol' Sherlock Holmes, eh?"

"No, Da—'"

"*Jennifer, listen to me as carefully as you possibly can: do not just pull random documents out of a stack and hold them up in the air. JEN. KINS.* What else?"

"Me?"

"Yeah."

"It's just one class at a time, every three weeks we switch."

"Sounds like a vacation. *It is a forty-five page bound book that says 'Building a Marketing Strategy for A New Decade' on the cover, which is not red, like the one*"

*in your hand, but black, like none of the presentations
you have held up yet."*

"Hello?"

"I'll tell ya, B. R., if you want to do something
right, you have to do it yourself."

"I know, Dad. Listen, I want to discuss something important with you." He took a deep breath, and
as proudly as he could, said: "I dropped out of the
business program at Middlebury last semester. I am
majoring in English."

There was a long pause.

"But Bale, you already speak English."

Ballon forced a laugh.

"Listen, Bale, money comes from hard work and
innovation. And there are two ways to continue the lifestyle you are accustomed to when I am gone: one is getting a job that pays an incredibly high salary and two is
taking up the family business, though I am skeptical at
this point that you'll have the focus and tools to take on
the latter, given what you are saying."

"But I feel there is mo—"

"I mean, how do you intend on supporting your
lifestyle? You need to understand that your life is only
possible because it is being paid for by me."

Bale missed an opportunity to interject.

"And where do you think I've gotten my money?
From hard, intelligent work. And it is getting *harder*. The
economy is moving towards the coffin. I can feel it. I
have the government breathing down by neck," he said,

adding: "I don't care what your *major* is—I care about results."

"I—"

"But listen, I gotta run, kiddo, say 'hi' to Sutton for me and tell him to lay off the sauce! *Jennniferrr—*"

His voice died and Ballon stared at the screen.

Bale picked up *Sons and Lovers*. Duffy commanded half of the book in a fortnight, as well as the other poems. He retreated through its covers, cowardly, indulgently; deeper into the literary forest he knew would hide him.

．　．　．　．　．

February 25, 2018

In South Kensington, weeks after their chance encounter, Bale sipped scotch and Meta a vodka with tonic, her wine-colored lips nibbling the straw. The waiter's boots skipped across the raw beef-colored hardwood. Meta tore a small piece of bread and used the squat knife to slash butter across it.

Their courtship had been flawless and fabulously sexual.

Discovery feeds intensity.

They drew closer over the dinners and coffees and drinks and museums and galleries and the one Chelsea football match that Meta barely agreed to attend but ended up loving. They had crossed the point of where two people tacitly agree there is no reason to end a relationship, which is of course the most wonderful and most dangerous stage.

"So you were saying about how living in the city is necessary, after you graduate?" he said.

"You cannot leave Manhattan. There is just no way to do it."

"Really?"

"L.A. is possible."

This was because of the demands of her burgeoning career and how she absolutely mandated to her agent and parents that she not be forced to choose between her acting career and completing school.

It is not necessary to document the nasty fights that had to take place between she and her mother, Sally, before she achieved that victory, but they were frequent and appalling.

It was her mother who first sought out her agent, Kyle Blunt, to help her teenage daughter find bigger roles, two Bale knew about: Audrey in *As You Like It* and Gwendolyn in *Travesties*, both far off Broadway.

"Blunt wants me to get into movies."

"But you prefer the stage?"

"I wouldn't *exclude* movies. It's just the adrenaline of live performance is incredible and American movies have become so jarring and flashy and convoluted."

"It's like being yelled at for two hours rather than being drawn in."

"Yes!" she said. "The *live* nature of theater raises the stakes and gives theater an *energy* that movies or TV can never have. I get as much of an adrenaline rush from the stage as I do from skiing or even rock climbing."

"For you is it the micro-control over what the audience sees," he said. "That you have stripped away the authoritarian nature of the editing process. And while of course a stage play is rehearsed and scripted and polished before an audience sees it, you are the one with the final say."

He loved these nighttime discussions about their futures and passions and ideas. He felt a freeness, a calmness with her in a way he had never felt at home, or with anyone, even with friends like Sutton. Like when you agonize for days over different options and finally settle on one. The stress and uncertainty disappear into confidence—it's as if you never had a doubt at all.

There was mutual respect and support. They needled each other in some ways—over miscalibrated ideas on politics or art or music—but what they were poking at was their meshing universes—making the whole of themselves stronger, more resilient.

She was equally awed by "the supple imagery" and "visceral elegance" in his poems he showed her and "disheartened and actually angry at how reserved they are," at times written as if "there was a shadow looming over you, or a peripheral crackup happening nearby that blurred your judgement." She encouraged him to trust his judgment and his voice. Ignore outsiders.

Eventually she told him—and he studied every line on her face as she said this to root out any forgery or agenda—"There is strength in writing, in storytelling, in easing your fellow human's misery, the aim of any writer. There is *greatness* in the act itself. There's a reason why, at weddings and funerals—the most important days of a person's life—people recite *poetry*."

Tisch was a nice compromise. She enrolled to placate her mother's insistence on craft-honing. Her father, the restaurateur Joseph Hadley, was against her going to university. His argument was that she was a precocious, talented woman who should not be exposed to the distractions of school, which would slow down an acting career. In other words, play as smartly and quickly as you can the hand you've been dealt.

He owned numerous upscale steakhouses all over New York and Las Vegas and Miami suburbia. He (and he had always been very clear that it was *his* money) had never gone to college and saw no point in it unless one wanted to do something that *requires* an advanced degree, such as lawyering.

He was a caricature of his own concocted image of an aristocrat. Slim, apart from a five-star paunch, quick-mouthed, unctuously dapper, and overly confident to the point of pomposity.

"Growing up without money," Meta explained, "he apparently thought it was very important not only to provide for us everything we could possibly need, but also to make sure he relentlessly made us aware he was doing so."

Bale understood this all too well.

But what Meta also really wanted, Bale learned on this date, "is a father who doesn't travel from city to city visiting his 'locations' and attending endless 'business meetings' about investment-type opportunities." Meta translated this, after finishing the last drop of her vodka, as lavish dinners and hotel-room-sex with girls only slightly older than she was.

Neither Meta nor her mother knew the full extent of the father's infidelity. But Sally knew enough between his random text messaging during the rare family dinner and credit card statements that showed hotel/room service bills that were too high for one person, even him.

Meta, who found out by seeing a raunchy text message on his phone when he left it face up on the hallway credenza, had never confronted him, though she often wished she would—her father's behavior worsened over the years as his wealth reached into the tens of millions of dollars.

She sipped from his scotch glass and told him both parents agreed to send her to the London program if she agreed to get "serious" about her career afterward. This was the compromise.

Bale admired how clear she was about what she wanted.

He could not, in the infancy of their relationship, describe to her the fear he felt—and that is unquestionably what it was—of ignoring or betraying his father's wishes.

Bastard or not, Bruce had always had a pull on his decision-making. He was larger than life. He survived the military as a Jew. Had a silent command of every room, every relationship, every interaction. What if he was right? Why not do what he said and be a banker for ten years? Have money socked away in case the wheels come off. A medical disaster struck. A pandemic.

And of course, Meta sensed Bale's thoughts on this by studying his eyes and the movements of his face, without him needing to say one word. She drained her vodka.

"The artist can never be afraid of failure. He must embrace failure like he does all emotion. He must encourage it, taunt it, and make it his own. And then crush it. All artists go crazy—because we are constantly forging and kneading and balancing within ourselves the entirety of human experience—but so what? Who gives a fuck about normalcy or even sanity? I've known you for only eight weeks and I don't need to see more to tell you that the only thing you need to do is to give expression to what is inside of you in the most honest and direct and uncompromised way you can."

After dinner they walked back over Millennium Bridge towards the Tube. When they were halfway across, Bale stopped on the bridge and told her, "It is hard to put in words how strongly I feel about you."

She kissed him.

Beyond them the only noise was the Thames pounding against the columns and shore rock piles and the faintest whisper of a restless, churning London.

THE BANK

Chicago: August 2019

7:45 a.m.

The office was empty except for Sherry, who was walking around in her socks slipping folders into storage drawers.

It was Thursday. Fifteen hours on Sunday, sixteen hours on Monday, nineteen hours on Tuesday, twenty-one hours on Wednesday. If he stayed on this schedule, he would reach a grand total of 103 hours for the week.

Sherry stopped by his desk, holding an armful of manila folders.

"You're in early."

"Haven't been home."

"You look like hell."

"Feel like it too."

"Hang in there," she said, adding, "we're all in

the same boat."

"Bad day?"

"Bad week. On top of the clerical bullshit I have to do, Escher now has me doing the pitchbook for Ag-tastic," Sherry said. "Said you guys can't handle any more work. Bunch of babies as far as I'm concerned."

She slapped his back and walked off.

He squinted at his screen. *Wait, that's so fucked up. She is now consistently doing analyst work and working these god-awful fucking hours and is not getting paid for it? He wondered to what extent the others knew or cared. Escher and Fredericks did, obviously. He wondered about Goldman.*

His desk phone rang. He recognized the number.

"Good morning," he said, "thank you for calling Goldman & Coli. Bale speaking."

"You sound so professional," his father said. "How are things over there?"

"Good. Listen, I am swamped. Can I call you later?"

"Yeah, of course. I wanted to check that we were still on for dinner tomorrow night. 7:30?"

"Yeah, of course," he lied. He forgot to make the reservation.

"Good. Feels like we haven't seen you in forever."

"Been working a lot, Dad."

"I know. I'm proud of you."

"See you tomorrow."

He stared blankly at his screens. *Feel slow. Too early. Coffee.* He walked to the front of the office, where

Sherry sat. He said to her: "I am going for a coffee. Would you like anything?"

"Latte."

He walked out of the building into the sooty August heat. When he walked into Starbucks, he saw Fredericks and McAllister and joined them at the end of the line.

"S'up, dude?" McAllister said.

"You look like my family's trailer park," Fredericks said.

"All-nighter," Bale said. "Hurricane's in Tampa and Goldman left for Saint Thomas for a little vay-cay. Only Escher and Sherry."

"One has the tits and the other has the shits," Fredericks said.

McAllister roared.

Bale was confused.

"*Dude, you didn't hear what happened?*" McAllister said.

Bale shook his head.

Bale and the other humans shuffled forward in the caffeine-injection line, many peering with tired eyes into electronic devices, or staring vacantly at the logoed thermoses and mugs and trucked-in processed nibbles and poverty-stitched furniture and focus-group-sanctioned artwork.

"So, we were at the closing dinner for the Focal deal. Place is packed. We finished three rounds of drinks and were starting on wine—and one of the executives tells this joke."

McAllister leaned into them and repeated it quietly:

"So, a husband and wife are fucking and in the middle of it the husband has a heart attack and dies right there on the spot. As the funeral arrangements are being made, the mortician informs the widow that he cannot get rid of her husband's rigor mortis, which is sticking into the air. He says if they don't do something, they won't be able to close the casket. The widow considers this for a moment or two and then tells the mortician to cut it off and stick it up his ass." They made silent exaggerated laughing movements.

"The mortician can't believe what he heard and protests—but the widow is adamant. So, the mortician does it. During the funeral, friends and relatives exchange concerns as they see a tear stream down from the corpse's eye. But the widow assured them that there was no cause to be alarmed. And as the people are filing out, just before the casket is closed, the widow leans down and whispers in her dead husband's ear: "Hurts, doesn't it?"

They made silent exaggerated laughing movements.

"Everyone at the table erupted in laughter and Escher laughed so hard he shit his pants!"

"No fucking way," Bale said.

"He had to excuse himself right there and go to the bathroom," McAllister said. "He comes back about ten minutes later looking sweaty and, like, *off*. The meal carried on and after a few minutes I got up to go to the bathroom. It is one of those single-use ones. When I finished washing my hands and went to throw the towel away, I saw—I swear to God—a shit-stained pair of tighty-whities stuffed into the garbage can."

It was their turn to order espresso, and they were all laughing so hard they couldn't get the words out.

"I'll take a redeye," Bale said.

"Well done, little fella," Fredericks said, pleased with Bale's order: "Make that two, please."

McAllister and Fredericks pulled cash out of their wallets. Ballon opened Apple Pay.

"Jesus Christ, Ratcliffe," McAllister said, "will you get some fucking cash together?"

"Cash is dirty, outdated."

"Hundreds are clean," McAllister said. "You'll know one day."

"I got 'em," Fredericks said, handing the woman crisp currency.

Outside, Ballon and McAllister had a cigarette while Fredericks went upstairs to the office. When they finished smoking, Ratcliffe remembered Sherry's coffee.

"Ah shit," Ballon said. "Gotta run an errand."

"What do you have to do?"

"Go see your mother."

"Fuck you, man."

"None of your business."

"Now I am actually interested," McAllister said.

"Nothing, really. Shoeshine."

"We got shined up yesterday after lunch."

"Dude, it's nothing."

"Stop being weird."

"Latte for Sherry."

"*I fucking knew* it!"

"Come on."

"D'juh fuck her yet?"

"No, man. Of course not. Did you know Escher is having her doing fucking analyst work?"

McAllister ignored him. "Don't think I didn't notice what's going on. Walking through the bullpen to tell you your phone messages in person instead of just emailing them, like she does for the rest of us. We all see it, B. R."

"Don't you think that's fucked up—that that piece of shit is making her work our hours and not paying her?"

"Dude, you should let me fuck her. You'll fuck it up."

They roared.

"Come on, I'll get her coffee with you. We'll have another cigarette to tide us over till lunch."

2:42 p.m.

Bale's computer kept freezing up. He lost two model iterations. Deadlines loomed. He was close but needed a good hour with no interruptions. He said "fuck this piece of shit" out loud and within one minute the IT handyman appeared in his cubicle. Bale stood up and watched the man adjust settings, toolbars, codes, and nodes.

3:23 p.m.

Rothkauf appeared at Bale's desk.

Bale was pounding away at the keyboard, charting for Escher the growth of Stetson Systems Inc. against S&P 500 technology sector indices and the broader market. He was instructed to produce a single "crisp" aggregation.

He mentally scribbled his own sinusoidal heart rate over the datum within. It danced jaggedly up over the data.

"*Ratcliffe*," Rothkauf said. "Your fingers are shaking."

He spun around in his chair.

"I know, J. B. Can't get them to stop."

"Listen. Let's go to the club, take a schvitz and a shower. Something to eat—you'll feel much better."

"Give me 20 minutes."

"Okay. Meet you in the lobby in twenty-five."

Bale felt thirsty. He went to the office kitchen. Escher was in there meekly sipping green tea:

"Doctor says it's good for my stomach," he said. Bale smiled at him perfunctorily.

Escher wheezed.

"You alright?" Bale said.

"My stomach has been very bad lately. Saltines and this tea are all I can handle. Been very difficult for me, very painful. Doctors can't figure out what the problem is."

"Shame."

"It is hard to go all day without eating a proper meal. It really eats into you," he said, giggling.

Bale tried to block murderous thoughts.

"I am almost done with your chart."

"Thanks."

Bale turned to leave but Escher cut in: "Bale, I think it would be meaningful to see the analysis done not only for the S&P but also the other major markets around the world. The Nikkei plus a few others? See how Stetson Systems stacks up in the *global* technology marketplace."

He took a sip of tea.

"Escher, you'll have to explain to me," Bale said, with barely the deference an analyst should have to a firm's partner, "because I am relatively new here, why that analysis is relevant since Stetson Systems is a *private* technology firm that focuses on *institutional security* systems only in the *aerospace defense sector.*"

"I am glad you asked, Ballon," Escher said, leaning back against the countertop as if to stabilize the massive weight of his greatness. "You see, when you're in this business as long as I have been, you develop what I like to call 'Instinctual Dynamo'. You develop an instinct for what will impress people. You, Bale, however, can only see a foot in front of your face, like a fish in a river, while I can see the full landscape, like a bald eagle.

Piece of shit.

"OK," Bale said, "When would you like to see the chart?"

"Seven p.m., as I believe I said previously."

Motherfucking cocksucker.

"OK."

"It would also be great if you could edit the first ten pages of the executive summary I crafted for Steel Works, given your English background."

"Tonight?" Bale said.

"Please," he said, delicately blowing over his tea. "After that, just paste the financials in the Financial Overview section of the memorandum, which should be done, and hit print. I'll stop by your desk at seven to see where we're at."

We? Who is we?

He watched Escher touch his hand to his gut and grimace. Ballon nodded at him and left the room.

He promptly went to the bathroom, checked for other inhabitants, and unleashed a silent, mouthing diatribe.

"Goldman must've sent him to some bullshit leadership seminar or executive coaching nonsense conference like, 'How to Perfect Your Managerial Strategy,' or some fucking thing," he mouthed to the mirror. "Some ex-Fortune 500 asshole in his suit hawking knowledge via PowerPoint for ten thousand dollars an hour with some pseudo-academic banner like 'Management 101' and something with 'tenets' and 'knowledge trees' and other motherfucking horseshit."

"One of the tenets, for sure, was 'make your target subordinate feel as though they are making the decision. That *their* opinion matters—which, of course, it does not,' ha ha ha the ex-Fortune-500 cocksucker says into his shirt-pinned microphone."

4:45 p.m.

He wrapped his loins in the warm plush cotton and leaned his aching back against the hot marble wall of the steam room at the East Bank Club and inhaled the eucalyptus-infused fog.

Rothkauf sat adjacent, with his burly body pressed against the stone and one foot propped up on the bench. Sweat rolled down his belly; he rubbed his chest below a gold necklace.

"You know, Goldman demands that you shave every day," Rothkauf said.

Bale laughed.

"No, seriously—"

"Didn't go home last night."

"It will be out-pointed in your review if he sees you like this. They have razors here or we could go for a shave. I know a great place."

"Ok, thanks, Rothy, I appreciate this."

"No problem, bud."

"What'd you do before G&C?"

"Bio-tech start-up. D.C."

"Why'd you leave?"

"It went under. Couldn't get more funding for research."

"I see."

"Just think of G&C as a necessary stop along the way," Rothkauf said. "Paying your dues."

Bale considered this.

"Have you seen the movie *Casino*?" Rothkauf said.

"Of course," Bale said.

"Remember the scene where De Niro is eating breakfast with his partner and he says, 'You see this? This pisses me off, your blueberry muffin has more blueberries than mine?"

"Yeah," Bale said.

"So, he goes into the kitchen and tells the casino chef that he wants *every single* blueberry muffin that comes out of his kitchen to have the same number of blueberries. And the chef says, with an exasperated expression: 'Do you have any idea how long that will take?' *That* is our job, Bale."

"Ha, yes," Bale said, "except, except, then the chef would do an entire batch of perfectly scattered blueberry muffins and then Escher would say, 'No no, I want you to do it again but this time with *seven* blueberries each and make sure *each* is the *same size*.' And then the chef would do that and come back to De Niro who would say 'Ya know what? Just go ahead and do it the way you did it the first time.' *Then* that'd be like our job."

"Just a stepping stone," Rothkauf said before sipping from a cup of forty-five-degree, triple-filtered, electrolyte-laced water. "Just a stepping stone."

Bale considered that he had no idea exactly where this "stepping stone" should lead. He knew immediately this made him different than the others.

Showered and shaved, they were walking back to the office, and ran into a girl Bale went to high school with.

"Bale?!"

"Hey, wow, how are you?"

"Good. You? I didn't realize you were in Chicago."

They had overlapping English and math classes, as well as the same breaks his senior year. He hadn't thought about high school in a long time.

"I work a few blocks from here at Goldman & Coli. This is my colleague, J. B."

They shook hands. Bale liked how she looked. Seemed happy, energetic, free.

"What do you do there," she said, without sufficient interest to merit a question mark.

"Mergers and acquisitions."

"Oh, cool. My mother is waiting for me outside. But listen, take my number. Celebrating my birthday this Saturday. Maybe you can come?"

"Sure," he handed to her his iPhone and she typed her number and handed it back.

"Bye!" she said, hopping away.

"What is she so goddamn happy about?" Rothkauf said.

Bale observed the bank-learned cynicism leaping from him.

"You need to join a place like this, Bale," he continued. "To escape the drudgery of your meaningless life. I'll give you a reference. There is an initial fee, which is massive, and then a monthly fee of only a few hundred dollars."

6:45 p.m.

Ballon was "finalizing" for Escher his chart in Excel so that the background of the graph was not shaded because he thought the white space behind the thin, colored lines allowed the information to appear crisper, like a billboard advertisement.

The Hurricane told him this made the data "jump out at ya."

He tried adding some dash marks that birthed on the Y-axis and ticked across the set, cleanly bisecting the jittery fluctuations of his index lines, but then realized it would be too much movement. He made sure the text on both axes was the same size and font and created a title that was simple but strong.

Fredericks stopped by and delivered a carved brick of chocolate cake. Bale looked at the pile of food and the fat-lubed disposable plate and grimaced.

"There you go, little fella," Fredericks said, chortling. "Saved you a little bite."

7 p.m.

"Hey, there," Escher said. "How's our analysis coming?"

"Finished the first set as well as the language modification. Need to start on the additional analysis."

"Oh, OK. I thought you'd be further along by now. I have to go see my doctor tonight, so I need to be on the 8:15 train."

"OK. I'll keep trucking on this and I should have something for you to review by then."

"And the pitch, too, right?"

"Yes."

Bale began constructing indices from the Nikkei, the FTSE, and the DAX.

7:45 p.m.

"How's it going?" Escher said, looking at his watch.

"Good. Nearly finished with the graphs."

"I have to leave."

"I am sorry. Do you want me to courier this to your house?"

"No. I wanted it done. But I will wait. I will catch the next train and call my doctor. He comes to my house so he will just have to come later."

Escher left.

Bale rubbed his eyes. He took the plate and stood up and walked it to McAllister's desk and found him on the phone with his girlfriend arguing about dinner plans and placed the plate down. McAllister let out a mirthless smile, acknowledging his presence, and then went back to her choice in sushi restaurants.

The formatting was taking longer than expected because of some insuperable deformity in Excel. One shouldn't have to compromise with one's technology.

His phone rang. It was the Hurricane.

"This is Bale."

"B. R. ... Jim Cross," the Hurricane said, pausing to let the full measure of his name permeate Bale's mind.

"Hey, Jim. Just saw your bonefish photos. Amazing."

"Aren't they? Landed twelve fish the first day. Just beautiful."

"Absolutely."

"What's going on there?"

"Working on some index analysis for Escher. And finalizing a pitch."

"Indices?"

"Tech companies."

"How are you weighting it?"

"By market cap."

There was a pause. Ballon put Cross on speaker-phone.

"Do it well," Cross said. "Listen, I am in the air right now. Got my wife and kids with me."

Bale heard Fredericks's voice starting in on something so Ballon lunged towards the phone and hit the mute key just in time.

"That means he is getting massaged by hookers in the back of a business jet."

The bullpen roared. Ballon exhaled.

"...I got a handful of companies that I need you to do some research on," Cross was saying. "Pull their profiles, news articles, research — et cetera. You with me?"

Bale slapped the mute key, "*Absolutely,* J. C., no problem." Bale winced over the ridiculous abbreviation.

"Good man," Cross said, apparently with approval. "Need it for tomorrow morning. Goldman and I are going after some companies in the healthcare staffing space. Meetings in the afternoon—"

Ballon took notes on his phone.

"—Anyway, I'll get you up to speed when I get in. We'll sit down about it."

Then the call went dead. He felt a presence behind him and turned to see Escher, visibly annoyed, standing behind him with a stack of papers.

"Analysis done?"

"Finished the charts. I will print them for you to review. In the meantime, I need to review the financials and put them into the pitch and edit your executive summary and drop it in."

8:38 p.m.

"It's 8:38 p.m., Bale," Escher said, back again at Bale's cubicle. "I wanted to be home by nine to meet with my doctor on my stomach cramps."

"You can go," Bale said. "I can finish up this work and have Fredericks or McAllister review it and have it on your desk by the time you come in tomorrow."

"No," Escher said. "I need to make sure it is correct this evening and suggest needed improvements. That is why I wanted it earlier. You'll do all that final reviewing and formatting afterward."

"OK. I'll get it done quickly as I can."

"OK. I'll be in my office."

Some minutes passed.

While reviewing the financial information he saw that the income statements had not included the most recent audits.

So he thought for a moment, then took his composition notebook and a pen and went down the corridor to Escher's office. The door was closed, so he knocked. He heard a muffled voice and entered. He saw on Escher's computer screen reflected in the building windows behind him that Escher was shopping on Amazon.

"Done?"

Bale spoke fast. "I know you have a train to catch and that you wanted to leave earlier. I am sorry for that. I have an idea."

Escher blinked at him.

"I looked at the financial section and it does not

have the latest audited financials. I can spread them and get it up to date and give it to you to review. The charts are done."

Blink blink blink blink.

"If you can review that portion now and then drop them into the presentation, I will push ahead on the rest. Like I said, I am sorry that this is all taking me so long—but this will get you out of here in half the time—if we team up. Divide and conquer," Bale said, smiling.

Escher swiped his palm languidly across his mahogany desk and rubbed his fingers together to expel a phantom pod of dust.

"*No*," he said. "You do all of it."

"That is, of course, fine," Ballon said quickly, thinking perhaps he didn't explain properly the true brilliance of his idea: "But if you would just review the charts and drop them in, I can finish the financials, edit the exec sum, and then print them. It'd be much faster—and plus I just got several hours more work from Jim to do in advance of a meeting they have tomorrow afternoon."

"Let me see if I can explain this to you differently," Escher said. "I want you do *everything* I asked you to do and when you are done, *I* will review it, *I* will suggest the appropriate changes, and then *I* will go home."

"Fine," Bale said, failing to mask his annoyance. He pulled Escher's massive mahogany door with an effort he thought would be loud and shattering but because the door was so large and dense and gorgeous it closed without much effect.

10:28 p.m.

The clicking of keyboards, guttural groans and throat-clears, and whirring of printers echoed throughout the bullpen. Rothkauf scooped up his ringing desk phone and engaged in muffled chatter for several minutes and then unleashed a volley of barrel-chested Ha-Ha-Has.

Rothkauf's email arrived to the other bullpenners seconds later. Fredericks quickly emerged from his cubicle in the center of the bullpen.

"Please note the time of J.B.'s email. *10:36 p.m.* After a one-hour schvitz *and* dinner and *then* another *two hours* of personal calls, Rothy finally sent out a work-*related* email. Not work, but *related.*"

Fredericks went back to his desk. Laughter faded, work resumed. After another twenty minutes, Fredericks shoved in his chair and said:

"See you queers tomorrow," and sprinted out for his train.

Bale went to see J.B.

"Isn't saying that shit in an office really messed up?" Bale said.

"Totally," Rothkauf said, laughing. "But you know how they say, 'if you can't beat 'em, join 'em'? You'll *never* beat them. And you can always pretend you haven't joined them."

Ballon was proud of himself. He handed Escher a mint presentation and got back a "good job" with a smile.

Some minutes later McAllister came to his desk.

"How you doing, Balfour?"

"Hanging in there."

"You got time later to help me print and bind some pitches?"

"'Course," he said.

"Thanks, dude."

Minutes later, Escher came back, announcing himself with a knock on Bale's cubicle wall. Ballon alt+tabbed away from his personal screen to an Excel model instantly, as analysts learn to do when they hear someone approaching their cubicle. Escher held the presentation with several sticky notes jetting out of the edges.

"Make these changes. Mostly small. Then print and bind six copies for me. I'll be in at 8:30 for a call and then I leave at 9:15 for the pitch."

He left.

Bale started on the changes. As soon as the side exit door banged closed, McAllister came to his desk.

"Before you print this shit, let's get in a game of Wall Ball."

"Three dollars a point."

"Ten dollars a point and drinks Friday night."

"Agreed."

They jogged and took their respective positions at either end of the long corridor that extended for about a hundred feet between the conference room and the entrance lobby.

The game's rules were simple. Hurl a tennis ball past your opponent who tries to stop it, goal-keeper style. McAllister threw first — three serves per turn — and pinged the tennis ball off two walls so that it ricocheted down to the ground between Bale's legs. He failed to trap it beneath a plummeting thigh.

"Fuck yah!"

But Bale returned with a knuckler that walloped off the wall above McAllister's left shoulder, which he could only block by driving his wiry frame into the dense sheet rock.

They wove in their typical assortment of change-ups, bouncers, and low-slung speed shots. After a taxing stalemate, they took two sets apiece and were tied going into their last serves.

McAllister, resting his palms on his scuffed trousers' knees, readied himself to serve. He shoved off the back wall with his foot, like a swimmer, for power, wind-milling his arm around his body and hurled the ball towards the ninety-degree angle where the wall and ground met beneath Bale's aching leg. McAllister hoped it would create a quick double bounce to the opposite wall, slipping by Ballon's misplaced lunge. But Bale anticipated the tactic and threw his entire body painfully into the wall, snuffing out the ball, which bounced off his groin and died.

"Fuck!" McAllister said.

"*Big mis*s," Ballon gasped. The wind was knocked out of him and he felt needles in his testicles.

Bale collected himself and took deep breaths. *This* was his moment. He had to give it everything he had.

In slow motion, he brought his body together in the form of a flagpole. He stared at his feet. Cleared his mind. He lifted his face and glared into McAllister's eyes. Then Bale lurched into motion, spinning his knuckles at the last moment to impart whirling spin, sending the projectile down the corridor only inches from the ceiling. McAllister licked his lips and readied to jump and smack it down, but at the last moment, the ball, which had been expertly released, ricocheted off the ceiling and jetted past McAllister's swatting palm. The popping thwack of the ball hitting the wall behind him echoed across the office.

"*Fuck yeah!*" Ballon said, pumping his fist.

"Fuck."

"Drinks on you, Bitch!"

"Fuck you."

"Only down one game now?"

"Let's bind some books."

11:17 p.m.

Bale had no phone messages and no emails, which was so strange that he triaged his Internet connection to be sure his systems weren't down.

Just a text from that Katzman, undoubtedly

slumped, disdainful and muscley, inside his claustro-
phobic JPMorgan cubicle.

[11:19:26 PM] Brad Katzman: god damnit ratman u christ killer motherfucker!

[11:19:38 PM] Ballon Ratcliffe: ha. leaving the office yet?

[11:19:45 PM] Brad Katzman: what are you kid-
ding? I'm just warming up.

[11:19:58 PM] Ballon Ratcliffe: hahahaha

[11:20:04 PM] Ballon Ratcliffe: what your hours
like these days

[11:20:15 PM] Ballon Ratcliffe: ?

Bale alt+tabbed between his buyers list and
the chat.

[11:20:36 PM] Brad Katzman: 9-2am

[11:21:09 PM] Ballon Ratcliffe: daily?

[11:21:15 PM] Brad Katzman: yes, and 10-10 on
the weekends

[11:21:26 PM] Ballon Ratcliffe: jesus. mine aren't
as bad. you get paid more tho

[11:21:29 PM] Brad Katzman: the money is epic.
Lots of zeros. Stacks and stacks of chips. But yah hours
real bad.

[11:21:41 PM] Brad Katzman: some weeks you
just don't leave, just shower at the company gym. 12th

floor. nice facility. Sleep on a couch.

Bale inadvertently discovered a formatting inconsistency in the E and F columns along the 126th row and called out: "How is that possible?"

He had been over the thing twelve times.

Bale went to correcting the formatting in the cells. Ctrl+c'ing over the cells he liked. He paused, watching the little pulsing border march around the cell's border, like ants around a mound. He felt a drop of sweat exit his arm pit, sending a little damp chill to the bones of this rib cage. It made him think of something. He texted Brad.

[11:24:36 PM] Ballon Ratcliffe: what is your mental state?

[11:24:36 PM] Ballon Ratcliffe: overall stability?

[11:24:45 PM] Brad Katzman: i am losing it.

[11:25:22 PM] Ballon Ratcliffe: haha

[11:25:36 PM] Brad Katzman: no serious nyc IS MAking me crazy...

[11:25:54 PM] Brad Katzman: the other day i almost jumped over the counter at Starbucks. i literally had to restrain myself.

[11:26:13 PM] Ballon Ratcliffe: hahahaha.

[11:26:23 PM] Brad Katzman: not funny dude. i feel like I have to run down the street everywhere. even when i have time, i find myself always in this sort of half-run.

Ballon alt-tab'ed back to Excel and, after checking that the cell was still blinking, maneuvered the box to the base of the bad cells and held Ctrl while he used the arrows to stretch the box over the badly formatted cells and then keyed Alt+E+S ("Paste Special") and pasted the formats over the cells.

[11:28:21 PM] Ballon Ratcliffe: do you have to dress up every day?
[11:28:26 PM] Ballon Ratcliffe: like tie
[11:28:29 PM] Ballon Ratcliffe: suit
[11:28:39 PM] Brad Katzman: yea
[11:28:42 PM] Brad Katzman: business FORMAL
[11:28:57 PM] Ballon Ratcliffe: sucks

McAllister called from his cube: "You ready, Ballous?"

"Two minutes," Bale said.

Bale read a pop-up message regarding his Windows Operating System. He re-read it. He hit cancel—a gamble—then waited. No disruption.

[11:33:03 PM] Ballon Ratcliffe: what is your caffeine intake?
[11:33:24 PM] Brad Katzman: continuous.
[11:34:13 PM] Ballon Ratcliffe: diet coke?

[11:34:22 PM] Ballon Ratcliffe: coff?
[11:34:26 PM] Ballon Ratcliffe: ?

The ideal analyst quickly arrives at the point where he is engaged in fluid action and equal reactions. So, at this point, true delays were caused by insufficient mental acuity (rare), misinterpretations or changes in top-down work requests (frequent), and computer hiccups (17.16 minutes of daily software delays, password re-entries, freezes, *et cetera*).

[11:37:23 PM] Brad Katzman: o my god.
[11:37:26 PM] Ballon Ratcliffe: what??
[11:37:36 PM] Brad Katzman: this cant be right.
[11:37:53 PM] Brad Katzman: i just got an email request from my M.D... hang on.

Ballon watched the buzzing curser and imagined the electrical pulses creating it. It looked like it was breathing. He matched his breath with it.

[11:39:00 PM] Brad Katzman: o. my. god. i just got a request that says to compute dividend payouts and fcf yield for the entire s&p 500.
[11:40:45 PM] Ballon Ratcliffe: holy. shit.
[11:41:50 PM] Brad Katzman: he says it has to be pro forma and adjusted for all extraordinary items.
[11:41:56 PM] Ballon Ratcliffe: no factset or capitaliq.

Bale just paused with his fingers suspended over the keys, his mouth gaped over the task. He visualized Brad strung out on caffeine and ambition in his cubicle. His pinstriped suit snug against his stout body. His eyes wide and puffy, skin pale from lack of natural UV exposure, Katzman was probably just staring at his computer screens in a where-do-I-even-fucking-start befuddled malaise.

11:45 p.m.

Bale was approaching two days without sleep. He alt+tabbed to his Excel screen, stood, and went to McAllister's cubicle where he was ardently attempting to remove a scuff from the right side of his Ferragamo penny loafers.

"Ready."

"Cool. OK. I will hit print on fifteen books in about five minutes. I am checking them once more. Go and set up the tabs and cover so we can fuck this thing assembly-line style."

"Cool."

"Hey, wait. Check this out."

McAllister alt+tabbed to YouTube where he found a scene in *Snatch* where Tyrone and Vinny were in a stolen car outside of the bookmakers. They watched it laughing.

"OK, Dude. Hitting print shortly."

The act of binding books required sustained mo-

notonous physical movements, coordination, and as-
siduous attention to detail—surprisingly difficult on little sleep.

As Bale laid out the tabs along the cabinet and
edged them into neat piles, he had the one thought an
analyst is *never* supposed to think when binding pitch
books, let alone writing them: *What if they don't even
look at them during the meeting?*

He looked up and stared blankly, remembering
that Escher once referred to the pitchbook as a "leave
behind"—like a pile of dog shit on grass.

Ballon knew that these types of thoughts chip
away at one's sanity.

"How's things with Stephanie?" Bale said.

"Complicated by the fact that we live together,"
McAllister said.

Bale laughed but McAllister wasn't joking.

"It seems like she is constantly mad at me. She
issues what she calls 'constructive ultimatums.'"

"What does that mean?"

"Idle threats."

"What's the problem?"

McAllister paused in thought.

"I guess, from my perspective, it is like we are on a
trans-Atlantic flight headed to the south of France flying
first class and all we need to do is sit back and enjoy the
Champagne and hot towelettes and oven-warmed ca-
shews and then she says, 'Wait a minute, we are going to
Antibes? Didn't you know I *hate* Antibes? And will you

have to work while we are there? And when are we going to get married...' And I'm just like, 'I don't know, honey, I have no idea. Can't you just enjoy these first-class tickets and this great wine and the fact that I am an investment banker instead of a cattle rancher in bumfuck Canada, and perhaps not complain for like ten minutes?'"

"I see," Bale said.

"Yeah."

"Do you love her?"

"What?"

"Love her. Do you."

"Your concept of love weakens with age."

Bale was depressed by that.

"Check those pages."

Bale grabbed the first huge stack of pages, and began collating them on the file cabinet. In another few minutes, McAllister took another huge stack and joined the assembly line.

"Now we're rollin," McAllister said.

They worked in perfect coordination. Suddenly McAllister blind-sided him.

"Why'd you want to get into investment banking?"

Bale, searching for an acceptable lie, rambled about his summer internship at a hedge fund after London.

"So it's the money, then. But didn't you study underwater basket weaving or some shit? How'd you even get an interview?"

"My dad was in the Marines with the fund's managing partner."

"*Ah ha.* Who's the M.D.?" McAllister said.

"A guy named Blake Schepp," Bale said.

"You say that as if I wouldn't know who Blake Schepp is. He made the famous Cow Town trades in 2014. We studied his arbitrage model at University of Chicago. Made a fortune but decimated the cattle market. My dad and his cattleman's association buddies view him literally as Satan."

"You can't make any mistakes, dude," McAllister added.

"I know, man," Bale said. "Lots of pressure."

"No, *literally*, with those pages in your hands. Don't fuck them up."

1:02 a.m.

McAllister moved onto asking Bale about women and Bale's mind swirled over that last year since being back from London and graduating college and told McAllister that he and Meta "just drifted apart," which of course was transparently dishonest and utterly unacceptable to McAllister, who demanded a lengthy discussion, likely for no other reason than it would ease his own misery.

So Bale told him what happened.

INTERLUDE LONDON

February–May 2018

Spring. At the flat. 1 p.m.

Ballon, returned from a workout, was perched at his living room desk to work on a final essay about two poems by Seamus Heaney. Class was at half three.

The phone jiggled in his pocket.

"Hiya, son!"

"Hello, Father. How are you?"

"Sorry about last time, I was tied up at work."

"No problem," Bale said, and slid his chair back, angling his body to look outside, staring down upon the gated green. Rain pelted the windowpane.

"Did you get my email, Dad?"

"What is it with you kids and email? Whatever happened to picking up the phone and calling someone? This lousy Jennifer at the office, she's about two years older than you, she sits at her desk and will go back and forth with Tim Brenner over email for *days*.

Tim sits about twenty feet from her desk. I keep telling her, pick up the damn phone and call the guy or better yet, *walk* over and have an *actual* conversation."

"Couldn't agree more, Dad. Listen, how's Mom?"

"O, Mom, well, Mom's not feeling, wait, she's grabbing the phone from me¬–"

"Hi, Honey, you're on speaker phone!" Ruth said, chipper as ever.

"Hey, Ma."

"How are you, honey? How is everything?"

"Wonderful. Studies are going very well."

"Oh, good!"

"Spending a few hours a week at the newspaper. Lots of marginalia but I do get to write up the occasional book review and will soon get to write a weekly roundup of off-West End theater. They asked me to do a feature on Andrew Motion, the poet."

"Oh, *wonderful*! I've seen your stories online! You're famous!

"Ha ha, thanks, Mom. "I just turned in this story about a guy who was arrested in Fishguard for spiking several of his wife's cigarettes with methamphetamine without telling her."

"Oh, my."

"*Right*? She smoked two on her way to work and then began panicking and drove herself to the hospital. The husband told police that spiking her cigarettes was the first step in his secret plan to slowly, systematically get his wife addicted to methamphetamine."

"Oh dear, that is just terrible! Well, it seems like you are having fun."

"I am."

"Your mother was telling me about your girl-friend—Meta, is it? That she lives in New York and is try-ing to be an actor?"

"Yes, Dad, she's wonderful. I think we are falling in love."

"That's *wonderful*, honey," Ruth said.

"Ah, that's nice" Bruce said. "What a wonderful feeling. Have you two talked about what's going to hap-pen after the semester ends?"

"We haven't really talked about it yet."

"There is no chance you'd be moving to New York then after graduation, though, right?"

"Oh, Bruce, lay off him!"

"I mean, that wouldn't exactly be fair to your mother and me, not least of all since I've told Blake Schepp about your aspirations and he's already lined up a job interview when you are back."

"Plenty of jobs in New York," Bale said flatly.

"Bruce, *honestly*—"

"But your first move out of college is crucial to your overall trajectory. Where are your connections? Your friends? Your family? You don't make a major life decision like this based on some *fling*."

"Bruce, it is outrageous to discuss this right now. He just said they haven't even discussed it."

"That's why it is the best time to bring it up. Is

there a chance she'd be willing to come to Chicago?"

"I couldn't ask her to do that, Dad, No. The acting universe is New York and Los Angeles."

"Well, we are *thrilled* you are having fun together," Ruth said.

"I can see that from your credit card statements," Bruce added.

"We miss you," his mother said. "The house seems so empty without you."

"Listen, I am so sorry, but I have to go and finish my poetry paper."

"I know a poem," Bruce said.

Bale laughed.

Bruce launched:

"Breathes there a man, with soul so dead,
Who never to himself hath said,
This is my own, my native land!
Whose heart hath ne'er within him burn'd,
As home his footsteps he hath turn'd
From wandering on a foreign strand!
If such there breathe, go, mark him well;
For him no Minstrel raptures swell;
High though his titles, proud his name,
Boundless his wealth as wish can claim;
Despite those titles, power, and pelf,
The wretch, concentrated all in self,
Living, shall forfeit fair renown,
And, doubly dying, shall go down
To the vile dust, from whence he sprung,

Unwept, unhonour'd, and unsung."

"*Good Lord*," Bale said. "When did you learn that?"

"In the Marine Corps. They made us memorize it. So we knew what a traitor was."

"Unbelievable."

"This is about a man who has deserted his country, a spy or something like that. *Or-r-r*, a son who has left his homeland, selfishly thinking about his own pleasure, leaving his mother and father behind."

Bruce's laughter was wild; Bale and Ruth were silent.

．　．　．　．　．

Late May. Classes were finished. Some of the *Guardian* journalists had organized a farewell party for Bale and another retiring writer at The Gunmakers, a small pub near the newsroom. After that Ballon rode the tube back to South Kensington, his mind abuzz from the chatter and beer.

The flat was dark when he entered; the roommates were out. He checked his phone and saw a text from Sutton with directions to a new club. "Remember Cassius!" Sutton added. "He that cuts so many years off his life, saves that much time fearing death."

Bale smiled. He loved his friend. But he had business to finish.

As a prop to give himself confidence, he unfurled

from his pocket his final essay for Dr. Duffy, written on T.S. Eliot's *The Waste Land*. He felt as he wrote it not just the culmination of a semester's sacrifice and achievement, but the genesis of what could possibly be a thesis-length work or—conceivably—the seeds of a writing career. Given what Dr. Duffy had said about his grading standards, the bold letter written in red at the top corner was so empowering to him he could scarcely look at it.

He plopped himself on the couch and called home.

"Hello?"

"Father."

"It's late there."

"The paper had a farewell party for me tonight, I've just gotten home."

"Fun?"

"Fun, yes. Wonderful. Dad, they offered me a job on their Sunday edition."

There was a pause on his father's end, which Bale figured had to do with the distance between them.

"That is something, B. R.," he said quietly.

"Yeah, the editor-in-chief asked to see me as I was leaving and gave me an offer."

"What are the terms?"

"The terms are a job at one of the greatest newspapers in the world."

"I am asking what they'll pay you."

"Well it's just a junior reporter position so..."

Bale remembered, during his third week working for Dr. Duffy's ex-pupil, the emotion that almost overwhelmed him as he bought a copy of the *Guardian* at the tube station kiosk at 5 a.m. in his sweatpants and popped it open to see his first byline in irrevocable print.

"It's an actual *job offer*," Bale said, trying again. "I was in shock."

Bruce was silent as Bale went on, which terrified Bale because he knew it meant a devastating chess move was coming. He could see his father's face. His mouth twisted into a foul toothy grimace as his son gushed misguided enthusiasm.

"Bale, I think it's a fine idea. Congratulations."

"Yeah, Dad? *Really*?"

"Absolutely son. *Absolutely.*"

But Bale could detect the malice in his father's voice, in the way only a family member can. His father clearly was enraged at how wayward, unrealistic and unambitious he believed his only son had become. How uninterested — or was it unimpressed? — in his own father's business success and the lessons he had fought so hard to impart. How his son did not recognize his debt.

"The best way to get what you want is to plan out how to achieve it," Bruce said. "Like anything, there may be obstacles. For example, the cost of living, Bale, not merely in London or this semester but your entire life. I mean, think of your private schooling and college education, credit card bills along with your tuition and board and car insurance and cell phone bills, et cetera, plus this month's credit card bill of twelve hundred pounds, what if you had to pay that off yourself? What if we cut you off right after this conversation, just to see what it means to be self-reliant? I mean, it can be very difficult to keep up with it all."

Bale imagined his father's hands shaking over printed pages from his credit card statement.

"Yes, dad, I understand that. I'd finish up my last year at Middlebury and then come back to London. I would definitely need to share an apartment far outside Kensington, ha ha ha," Bale said. "Live simply, carefully. Work on my writing."

Bale illuminated his grand plans for some time before pausing to hear Bruce's response. His father spoke softly and evenly, though his gargantuan breaths told Bale spiteful rage was rising inside of him.

"Your naivete and your narrowmindedness is *absurd*. It doesn't just threaten your future, it threatens everything I have created and it undermines the investment we've made in your future. It threatens *my* name."

"But Da—"

"We didn't send you to Loftman and Middlebury and London so you could sit around all day writing fucking poetry like some goddamn weirdo hippie. We did it so you could make something with your life and do *better* than we did."

"Da—"

"And this fucking *girl* you are seeing is *poisoning* tha—clouding your already weak judgment."

"Da—"

"Given how complex you've made everything, I

have thought long and hard about your situation and you leave me no choice. I've decided to make this super *simple* for you: Give up this London nonsense. Come back to Chicago. See Schepp about working at the hedge fund this summer for an internship. Or I'll cut you off from this family."

After they hung up, Bale stared out of the living room window at the foggy green laced with moonlight.

Beside him lay his rumpled essay and its grandiose scarlet letter: "A."

· · · · ·

A full moon shone upon a little restaurant patio where Meta and Bale sat and ate tajine.

The countdown of their hours had ticked down to the end. It was their last night in London, their last meal. Meta had been talking about a script she had seen by a beautiful writer—"they didn't have to change a single word"—and Bale continuously had to beat back feelings of confusion and misery at what he saw as his life's unavoidable new trajectory.

Bale was surprised when Meta said, suddenly: "Couldn't you live like this forever?"

His brain, twisted and belittled by his father's manipulative cynicism, darkened her words — which were chosen and delivered with no more significance than to celebrate a single beautiful moment — into a mean challenge that dangled in front of his face the very thing he could never have, and then yanked it away.

He smiled, she saw that. He rubbed his clammy palms under the table as he tried to chart out a response, or perhaps what questions to ask, or how to bury the nagging humiliation of the relatively little he now felt he offered her, and the unanswered questions, not just about what she really wanted in a lover but what she expected out of him as a companion, or possibly a husband.

He thought of the only husband he knew well, clamped down at his desk, needling some report while his mother sat in her desk alcove filling her calendar with various fundraisers, book parties, and independent film screenings. How miserably his father had let her down.

Bale had spoken to his mother the day after his father's threat, though he couldn't pry from her a clear answer on what he should do. She just kept repeating that it was "such a *terrible* situation." She acknowledged that she partially saw Bruce's point—on the powerful nucleus of Bale's Chicago circle—though she also worried about the impact that a father-son cataclysm would have on her own relationship with her son. His father was *stubborn*, yes, but he *means well* and *loves you*. You are still *so young*, and *give it time*, and *talk to Meta*.

But in that moment, he saw something so repulsive and risky about dragging Meta into this new melodrama—it would irreparably ruin her already skeptical view of Bruce's character, while at the same time revealing which rung of the ladder Bale had placed her on.

Regardless he *knew* the right words to say to Meta. He had thought of them countless times, waiting for the precise moment, and now on this glorious patio he could just come right out and scream it:

Yes, I *do* see us like this forever. *I love you.*

But he didn't say anything.

And immediately his delay and vacant stare suggested to her a much deeper problem. Had she misinterpreted his feelings these past few months? How could the mere suggestion, even if it wasn't intended, of sharing his life with her be met with such callous blankness?

They searched each other's body for answers.

He was lost in that terrible mode of overthinking — when so many words crowd the mind that you can't pick a place to start. It was as if he was a wounded, frigid little boy vanquished on that bluff of their house as his father stood over him shaking his head disapprovingly.

Bale looked into her eyes and watched them flare for an instant, as a candle gasping for air, seeking an oxygen source he did nothing but suffocate.

THE BANK

Chicago: August 2019

1:03 a.m.

And so Bale told McAllister how Meta and he were on two distant paths after London: New York City for her, and Chicago for him, for the summer, and then off to senior year of college and then his job at the bank, post-graduation.

The misery was compounded, Bale told McAllister, as he followed her expanding life via social media—jetting between L.A. and New York for auditions or shooting or performances—while Bale sucked down shitty beer in pastoral Vermont while studying Black-Scholes graffiti.

"So she's like hot shit, then?"

"She is."

"*Wait*, dude, do I like *know* who she is?"

"Just hang on a fucking second, McAllister, and

let me finish the story."

"OK, dude, go head."

1:04 a.m.

"You can go home, McAllister. I can finish these up."

"No, no. Let's do them together. It'll be faster. I gotta deliver them personally to Hurricane's house anyway."

"OK."

Bale decided music would help ease the drudgery. He put a Spotify station on Sonos and strolled back to the binding room against the soothing beat of the Eurythmics' "Sweet Dreams."

McAllister began doing a little club dance by his books. Then he lifted his right leg up onto the lip of a potted plant's base and did a thrusting motion to the electronic beat. He called the move "The Pigou," after English economist Arthur Pigou who devised a system of taxes, price floors and ceilings.

McAllister also used the name in the crudest sexual manner, as in "Dude, I Pigou-ed the shit out of my girlfriend last night."

1:27 a.m.

The fifteen books were collated, bound, stacked—shimmering in the glare of corporate fluorescent lighting.

They both stood there, McAllister and Ballon

with their arms wrapped around their chests, looking at their creation.

"All right," McAllister said, "let's go through them."

Bale grabbed a stack and plopped them on the filing cabinet.

McAllister, stared at the larger pile of remaining books, and grew irate over his assumption that Bale was slyly trying to offload work on a higher-ranking associate.

"Don't be a Jew," McAllister said, grabbing the remaining books and dumping them on Bale's pile.

"What the fuck, man," Bale said.

"What the fuck what?" McAllister said, reaching for the pile.

Without thinking, Bale swiped McAllister's arm away from the pile, saying, "Why the fuck are you saying racist shit to me?"

McAllister shoved his arm down and stepped an inch from Bale's face. Bale shoved him back, but McAllister quickly grabbed two fistfuls of Bale's shirt and flung him up against the filing cabinet, causing a green potted plant to fall and shatter on the carpeting.

They clawed at each other, veins jumping out over the ruby skulls as they flailed and cursed and spit.

McAllister swung Bale toward another cabinet, which he slammed into, tearing his shirt from nape to waist.

Both McAllister and Ballon's eyes grew wide at the gashing sound and they instantly stopped fighting. McAllister rested his palms on his knees, panting as Ballon grappled with the back of his shirt to appraise the damage.

They both took seats on the carpet beside each other. McAllister leaned his skull against a cabinet. Bale cracked his knuckles.

They both knew the fight was about more than a slur, the difference was that McAllister didn't care. For Bale, in that moment it seemed as if all of American life boils down to an endless war between spitefully evil bastards and those trying to marginally disrupt their influence.

Johnny Cash's "Flesh and Blood" was now playing.

"Thisisagreatsong," McAllister said.

"Yeahitisman," Ballon said.

Flesh and blood needs flesh and blood, and you're the one I need.

2:45 a.m.

Ballon was alone. McAllister left twenty-six minutes earlier in a yellow cab bound for Hurricane's house with his fifteen immaculate books stowed in a padded compartment of his Tumi briefcase. He had given Bale elaborate instructions via email and voicemail to his residence—one of those rowhouse-type single-family homes that form the first levels of tall apartment high-rises in the Gold Coast.

He played Beethoven's "Moonlight Sonata" and turned off his monitors. In the blackened screens his face looked like a sack of potatoes. His armpit squeezed out droplets of sweat. He smelt of stress and rage.

He remembered he had to print and bind six books, separately, for Escher, who said the pitch was at 9:15 at their office, so the materials had to be finalized before Escher arrived around 8.

He turned back on his monitor.

7 a.m.

The loud sudden *whasssssp* of newspaper onto his desk woke him and he popped his eyes open and found McAllister standing in a black suit above him, grinning. Ballon smelled his eucalyptus after-shave and his extra-shot cappuccino.

"Did you bind your books?"

"Yes fucker, I was sleeping," Ballon said. He grunted and moved his stony legs and walked as best he could to the toilet where, teetering over the sink, he was dismayed at how outrageously horrible he looked, with white paste at his lip's corners and bloodshot eyes above great gray canyons of desperation and three fresh mega pimples on his neckline just below his jaw.

Was his urine *too* yellow? Was that merely acute dehydration or a harbinger of some greater internal sickness?

He fastened the elaborate system of his trousers and walked to the sink. He decided against washing his hands because, honestly, what's the point at this stage of emaciation?

He hurried back to his cubicle and grabbed his

wallet and unwrapped a spare dry-cleaned shirt from a package stowed in his desk. He walked out of the bull-pen, down the Wall Ball corridor, around a couple bends and past a conference room to the main lobby where Sherry's slowwwww head swivel and gaping stare said enough about his appearance. He walked out of the office, down the corridor and hit the elevator.

"You needed to change elevators mid-way down a skyscraper," J. B. Rothkauf once explained, "because a single elevator system that high would collapse under the weight of its own cables, from an engineering standpoint."

He always remembered this as he walked the corridors to change elevator banks and passed a row of huge windows, overlooking the city.

Sometimes, in the early hours of the morning, he would press himself to the glass, like a child peering into an aquarium.

He looked at the tight grid of Chicago and the little ant-like movements of people and cars and buses that give energy and meaning to its structures.

The perfect grid work and cross-hatchings, the X-axis of Madison Avenue and the Y-axis of State Street and the fucking non-linear streets of Elston Avenue and the Kennedy Expressway like $y=(x)(3)-x$, $2x+y=4$ and $y=x3$ tearing through the grid like ad hoc insurrections.

He saw Lake Shore Drive winding like a skinny estuary along the Lake Michigan beach and the cars' lights bleeding together like currents and silver cars changing lanes like shimmering salmon. Then the ale-colored beach and the water, spreading out like a hulking blue mirror materializing from the smoky horizon, whose whimsical spectrum burned around the sun, a keyhole into hell.

He asked himself, possibly out loud, if he was perhaps losing his mind?

His iPhone buzzed.

There was a news article about unemployment being up 0.2% for the quarter. Another said that in bad economic times alcoholism, suicides, and vasectomies increase. It follows, then, that alcohol, razor blades, and tube-tiers are counter-cyclical and elastic—and when people are worse off, the real cost of those products rises yet they buy more of them.

I shall call these products *Ballon Goods*, he mused.

He smiled and decided that he needed to move else he might fall asleep standing up, leaning against the glass.

He, a slowly dying organism, spent nineteen minutes a day going up and down gorgeous elevators and escalators.

Outside, his flesh sizzled in the muggy August daylight. A faint breeze waltzed down Wacker Drive and tickled his forearm, the way Meta used to. He shivered. He humped 3.23 blocks to a Starbucks on Wacker Drive.

The coffee needled his esophagus.

He saw the faces of the burnt-out, mobile-electrified commuters in sweltering pods.

He hailed a cab and fled to the front entrance of the East Bank Club, where he was now a proud member eagerly surpassing his monthly on-premise spending minimums and asking downtrodden employees to arrange massages and racquetball courts for him weeks in advance.

8:17 a.m.

The locker-room was buzzing. Bale shook free of his gashed shirt, put on his workout attire and went to the running track. He lapped it a dozen times, passing numerous pregnant bellies and aging marathoners, and then, on the way to the free-weights stopped to watch former U.S. President Barack Obama drive hard through a pack of pick-up basketball gamers.

Bale went back to the locker room, re-toweled, and went to the steam room. He stayed there until his lungs felt lubricated and his head de-throbbed and then he took a shower. He shaved in the common area where a puckered man was plucking his eyebrows and talking into his headset about options arbitrage, in clear violation of what Katzman called "Generally Accepted Locker Room Principles," or "GALP."

He checked his iPhone.

Emails were swelling in.

He stopped in the little East Bank Club Food Shop and got an enormous coffee and muffin. Then he asked for another laced with chocolate, to spike Fredericks.

9:51 a.m.

Ballon was making minute adjustments to the alignment of inserted Excel charts in PowerPoint slides. Fredericks stopped by on the way to his own desk. Bale eagerly got up and, giggling, placed the fat chocolate muffin that he had bought at the club and cut up into small pieces each adorned with a sliver of butter on the corner of his desk.

When Fredericks saw it, he roared.

"How did you know I like huge injections of chocolate in the morning?" Fredericks said. "I'll let my doctor know when he is addressing my cholesterol. I've built his career on trying to lower the reading."

"What's it at?"

"190."

"Is that good?"

Fredericks roared: "God you *are* young. No, 190 is terrible. It was 240 when I started working but I am on meds now and trying to control my diet."

"Anything to help."

"So let's powwow on this management presentation when you're done with those books."

"No prob."

Ballon, back to his cubicle, printed one book and studied a PDF called "3rd Quarter Transactions in the

Healthcare Industry." He populated it with quotes and links to articles and transactions. He hit ctrl+c over the text and then alt+tabbed to the Word Doc and hit ctrl+c.

It did not paste.

He wrinkled his brow and tried again.

Alt+tabbed to PDF, up-arrowed to the text, ctrl+left arrowed over it, ctrl+c'd it, alt+tabbed to Word Doc, down-arrowed to bottom of list, ctrl+v.

Nothing. He repeated this process eleven times without realizing it. A pop-up advert with several dancing smiley faces snapped him free of the repetition.

He crossed the point where "the aggressive use of the scientific method flirts with the clinical definition of insanity," as Fredericks described such behavior.

He manually typed the sentence describing the transaction in his Word Doc, hit ctrl+s to save it, and went to the backroom to check on his printing. The document was streaming out smoothly. He spot-checked two pages for ink levels and clarity. He returned to his desk and printed six more copies. He rapidly returned to the backroom where he began setting up his binding assembly line. He began collating.

10:23 a.m.

Back at his desk, Ballon was going page-by-page through the books checking for accuracy in binding. His phone rang; he sprang to it.

"This is Bale."

"Well, hello, my busy young professional and

how are we on this lovely Friday morning?"

"Mom, it is wonderful to hear your voice."

"We're on for dinner, right?

"Yes, of course, sorry it has been so long."

"That's OK, honey, we understand."

His iPhone vibrated once indicating a new email and he went to check his desktop. It was from Hurricane. McAllister was copied.

"Gents. Thanks for the late-night book binding efforts. Everything looks great. Appreciate your hard work."

Ballon smiled.

"Mom, I gotta go. Love you."

He got up and went to McAllister's desk. McAllister's face was about an inch from his screen; he was toying with the purchase price and structure of an LBO model.

He sensed Ballon's presence: "'Sup dude?"

"Hey. See Hurricane's email?"

"Yep. That guy is money."

"Seriously"—Ballon quieted his voice—"that is what I am fucking talking about, man. The guy is so busy, so overworked and overstressed and he *still* reaches out to us with a thank-you email. Absolute mensch."

"I know, dude," McAllister said.

The hushed expletives aroused the interest of Fredericks and J. B. who appeared in that order at the cubicle's entrance eagerly awaiting information.

"Who's fucking whom?" Fredericks said.

"We got a nice email from Hurricane, thanking us for our work," Ballon said.

"Good work, pud suckers," Fredericks said.

McAllister stood up and touched Ballon's sleeve: "New shirt?"

"Just."

McAllister laughed.

"I should fucking bill you," Bale said.

"I wouldn't pay it."

"Bastard."

"What happened little guy?" Fredericks asked. "You two have a little late-night sex-a-thon in the copy room?"

"A little scuffle."

"Maybe you two and Rothkauf should have a gay-down: whoever can choke the most athlete rope in an hour."

"Jesus," Bale said.

"We cool?" McAllister said, extending his hand.

Bale walked away, not taking it, and said: "You owe me drinks for my Wall Ball win. I'm free Saturday."

"B. R.," McAllister called, "look at this."

Ballon turned. McAllister had his leg up on his chair, *Pigou-ing* it. He then paused to pull up his sock.

"Money sock pull," Bale said.

Bale gathered the books on his desk and walked out of the bullpen, up the Wall Ball corridor to the office of Escher I. Coli.

9:26 a.m.

The massive mahogany door was closed.

Ballon knocked. No response.

Maybe he has a doctor's appointment this morning. No, no, he said he needs these by 9:30 a.m.

He turned the handle of the door.

He startled Escher, who had apparently forgotten to lock the door.

They froze.

Bale appraised the situation:

Behold, Escher I. Coli, Managing Partner of Goldman & Coli and pity-seeking sufferer from Crohn's Disease, sitting at his desk in his undershirt at 9:27 in the morning, stuffing his face with a "burritos-as-big-as-your-head" breakfast burrito and sucking out of a jug of Diet Coke with a combination of re-fried beans and sour cream globbed on the corners of his undulating mouth.

Ballon placed the books on Escher's desk as Escher made jagged, awkward movements and started an apology, spitting soggy flecks of rice out into the room. He was clearly mortified.

Bale was about to seize the moment, say something to gain even a moment of authority over a dour misanthrope who had openly sought to make his life miserable. But Bale remembered his mother telling him never to say something that might make a person feel worse than they already do about themselves, even if they deserve it.

"They make those things too damn big," Bale said, smiling as he handed Escher a napkin off the desk.

"They are delicious though," Escher said, smiling back.

. . . . .

Sunday. A sweet fog lingered like battlefield smoke over the Chicago business district. Bale approached the homeless man sitting on the marble ledge. Over the man's shoulder were a little green plot of grass below the Willis Tower, mortal green, slick with moisture, and a little shrub. Above that was 1,450 ft. of phallic steel.

The man had a sign now that said: "Homeless and Hungry. Please Help." His stained pants rolled up around tattered Florsheims with no socks.

Bale remembered the years of Thanksgiving and Christmas mornings his mother took him to deliver meals for Little Brothers—Friends of the Elderly at nursing homes dotting Chicago. She'd perch gingerly at dozens of bedsides and listen to stories of loss and poverty. The source of her compassion was her understanding that most of what determines a person's material success in this world comes down to things he or she can't control—where and when she was born, who her parents are, and her cognitive ability. The "dumb luck of the wealthy" in a system that enshrines privilege and inheritance for the few.

His father, however, believed it came from boot-strapping toil. The desire to claw one's way ahead of the bloodthirsty pack. Poverty and prejudice? Please, Bale's great-grandfather on his father's side—Isaac Siniouski—had stepped onto Ellis Island more than a hundred years ago, a *Jew* with a *few coins* clanging around in his pocket, straight off a *farm* near Chelm, Poland. At Ellis Island, an anti-Semitic immigration officer ignored his slow pronunciation and changed Siniouski to "*Rat*cliffe," or so the story goes.

Bale placed a dollar in the man's foam cup. The man grinned, flared his eyes and said "thank you." Bale walked on and lit a cigarette near the main entrance of the Willis Tower.

He thought of Oscar Wilde's declaration that a cigarette is the perfect indulgence because it is exquisite and never leaves one satisfied.

He looked at the Maurice Lacroix Masterpiece Chronograph his father gave him as a graduation present, which Bruce surely knew was *perfect* for the bank's obscene materialism. His father obviously thought it would help him to fit in.

3:37 p.m.

He used his key fob to unlock the office's main door. He flipped on the lights. The office was weekend-silent. The stale odor of post-vacuuming and lemon-scented wood finisher was subtly offensive.

He sat at his desk, with fresh rag-drag stripes across it, and turned on his computer. While it booted, he flipped through his composition book to a page titled: List of Potential Acquisition Targets for Optimix Envelope.

At 7 a.m. that same morning, he had received an email from Goldman. It said:

"Bale: Hope your weekend was great—

Ballon hung his head when he read the past tense: "was"

—Please go into the office. Go to my phone. Hit the illuminated voice-message button. The password is #4586. Listen to the message from Jake Schlockman from Optimix Envelope. He wants us to look at acquisition targets for him. He rattled off a bunch of names on the message. Listen to the message, write the names down, then do profiles of all of them. Shouldn't be more than a dozen or so. We'll talk first-thing Monday morning."

Ballon walked into Goldman's office. There was a vase of tulips on a circular meeting table, a row of framed family photos on his Prius-sized desk, and an antique standing bar holding a bottle of 67-year-old Macallan Lalique single malt. Not a speck of dust.

There was a ten-foot high bookcase filled with acrylic deal tombstones—little trophies of the deals he closed over his thirty-year career.

Bale scanned them: a 1991 capital raise for Mattel had a Micro Machine car on it. An LBO takeover of SwiftSteel from 1997 had a little crane hoisting steel beams. And an IPO for a tech startup named Veri-Soft, which about six years too early developed a video conferencing apparatus and went bust.

He picked up the phone receiver and envisioned that he was Goldman, chomping on a stick of gum after one of his salad lunches, ribbing an old country club friend over his stunted golf game. He looked out the massive bay of naked windows at the tremendous expanse of Lake Michigan and the heads of skyscapers.

He knew he was supposed to *feel* something at that desk. Power? Glory? Respect?

He felt lonely. And the view was better from a rowboat on a trout river.

He pushed the phone's lighted message button and when prompted, keyed in the password, pushed another button to slow down the speech and wrote down the names. There were twenty-eight.

Bale went to the kitchen, opened the fridge, and pounded a Diet Coke.

He returned to his cubicle to a chat message from Katzman detailing his latest Wall Street misery.

[4:15:32 PM] Brad Katzman says: things bad. been in office since Friday. i had to do 85 comps for a sum-of-the-parts valuation on Telstra.

[4:16:01 PM] Ballon Ratcliffe says: sorry man.

here too. gotta profile like 50 targets.

[4:16:37 PM] Brad Katzman says: brutal. funny story, tho.

[4:17:02 PM] Ballon Ratcliffe says: what happened?

Ballon launched Capital IQ and began Target Screening. He knew Goldman would want to see other names, besides the ones given by Optimix's CEO.

[4:58:44 PM] Brad Katzman says: i was here Friday night. This M.D. called me at 12AM screaming

[4:58:51 PM] Brad Katzman says: this is the head of M&A

[4:59:00 PM] Brad Katzman says: i put him on speakerphone so everyone could here

[4:59:15 PM] Brad Katzman says: * hear

[4:59:20 PM] Brad Katzman says: we all sat around my phone as he yelled at me that the valuation was lower than the range he told the client it would be and he then started asking me what the valuation was for all these obscure Asian telecom companies

[4:59:44 PM] Brad Katzman says: i'm just like, i have no idea

[4:59:56 PM] Brad Katzman says: he's like, well Brad, what do you suggest i do?

[5:00:17 PM] Brad Katzman says: I said, jokingly, why don't we just exclude the lower valued companies from the valuation to artificially make the company seem like it's worth more.

[5:00:22 PM] Brad Katzman says: and he goes, 'ok, do that'

[5:02:35 PM] Ballon Ratcliffe says: LMAO.

[5:05:21 PM] Brad Katzman: hahaha. We have contests we call feats of consumption, which involve eating the leftover food from meetings

[5:05:30 PM] Brad Katzman: this intern ate an entire cheese log in 30 minutes

[5:05:45 PM] Ballon Ratcliffe: hahaha

[5:06:11 PM] Brad Katzman: gave him diarrhea for two days.

[5:07:12 PM] Ballon Ratcliffe: hahahaha

[5:07:29 PM] Brad Katzman: i won the annual international JPMorgan water-chugging contest we video-conferenced with los angeles, london, frankfurt, and tokyo. there were twenty analysts competing, me and this kid phil were representing the new york office. I drank two liters of water in 80 seconds.

[5:07:44 PM] Brad Katzman: i vomited immediately afterward

[5:07:51 PM] Ballon Ratcliffe: hahahahahahaha

[5:07:54 PM] Brad Katzman: barely made it to the bathroom

[5:08:07 PM] Brad Katzman: i won the whole thing, 300 dollars, based on that day's currency exchange rates.

There was a pause in their conversation for a few minutes as Ballon needed to closely read three Capital

IQ-generated company descriptions.

A droplet of sweat fell from Ballon's underarm, made contact at the top of his ribcage and rolled down the ribs to his beltline.

"What the fuck," he said, and went to the kitchen, unbuttoning his shirt along the way and blotted himself with a paper towel. He returned to his desk and typed "unexplainable armpit sweating" into Google and spent several minutes in self-diagnosing misery.

. . . . .

7:15 a.m.

The following Friday, Ballon arrived first to the office. He was immaculately dressed, not a hair follicle askew, and not tired or hungry. And here was the strangest part: he didn't want even a sip of his espresso-spiked coffee.

His mind was elegant and eager, handling hyper-charged analytics w/o cumbersome abstract ruminative sidebars. His condition was mystifying.

He tallied the drinks he and Mara Shiffman, who he met at the health club, consumed before returning to her parent's vacant penthouse overlooking Lake Michigan:

> *1.* 2 Tito's and soda at James Hotel, Chicago. $26.
>
> *2.* 4 glasses of Soter Vineyards, "Planet Oregon"

2016 at RPM Italian. $56.

3. 2 Half Acre Daisy Cutter Pale Ales at Danny's on Dickens, $12.

Ballon smoked seven cigarettes from around the time of the 8:15 p.m. reservation to 12:30 a.m., particularly when the conversation swirled down the rabbit hole into gossip about Chicago's elite families and their offspring.

After dinner and Danny's, they took a cab back to her parent's penthouse. They flew East down North Avenue with the windows open, some sort of lyrical Berber music fluttering in the background. Mara draped her legs across his trousers.

They stumbled into the doorway, kissing and working their hands over each other. Ballon promptly backpedaled into a century-old writing table that held a Basque urn, which toppled and shattered, causing Mara to excuse herself to the bathroom to calm things down.

He stabilized and regarded himself in a hallway mirror.

Who *was* this deteriorating philistine destroying a museum-like 3,500-square-foot condominium with a gut full of liquor and steak on a Thursday at two in the morning?

Self-hatred piling up within his rotting tomb-mind, he walked through the massive rooms lined with oil paintings and mixed-media sculpture, Moroccan carpets and Herman Miller couches, through the chef's kitchen and out onto the flagstone patio to smoke a cigarette, his last.

Ah, his cigarette. His real, personal product, which he drew into himself with as much pleasure as happy disgust.

The breeze off Lake Michigan soothed his face. From the 24th floor, he saw the boats bobbing up and down in the harbor and he saw the cars blurring down Lake Shore Drive. He ogled the upper echelons of the Willis Tower poking above the buildings, like a child terrified of a horror movie but unable to avert his eyes.

7:16 a.m.

That debauch was only hours earlier.

His tasks that morning were like weightlifting exercises with too little weight on the barbell—each one simple and easy but taken aggregately, over many hours, damage-inducing.

He had to send out dozens of company sales memoranda to prospective buyers. Normally the thought of this phase of a company's sale alone was enough to make him swill caffeine. By nature, he reached for his coffee, but the smell made him queasy.

His caffeine intake was nearly continuous: two "grande" Starbucks redeyes (morning, late afternoon), Diet Cokes with lunch and dinner.

But his body didn't want the caffeine. Didn't need it. His fingers that were lighting up the keyboard.

His mind fired perspicaciously. He had achieved an inexplicable autopilot.

He thought that he should be *more* hung over.

Yes, there was the sour-sweet ammoniac taste of digested alcohol; his hands quivered as if possessed by some inward scabrous demon; and there was a fire in his head. But his body was allowing him to work unmolested.

It was true that beads of sweat cascaded from his soaked underarms, but not much more than normal, and his foot itched severely under his Ferragamo driving shoe (usually those shoes were only for weekends, but he changed before his date last night and, alas, didn't go home to reverse; Mara had rooted around her father's walk-in closet for a suitable shirt).

This itching marked a new ailment, a kind of obsessive-compulsive tick. The itching increased the more he clawed, like all life's top cravings.

All measures to alleviate this now-chronic skin problem had thus far failed. He began taking heaps of black socks to a dry cleaner in Bucktown that specialized in environmentally safe, organic methods. Hundreds of dollars in sock dry cleaning offered little help.

Then he tried wearing only *new* socks every day. He had no time for dermatologist visits, but had called the head of dermatology at Rush and had a video conference from his cubicle—after hours—explaining the nagging, painful itching. He held his foot up to the computer's camera to show the doctor the, scabby, beet-red condition that Fredericks despicably called "The Aids."

Despite all of this, Bale was in the zone. It was the first time since starting at the bank that he felt this productive—so unconsciously committed to labor that he had a stack of sixteen Confidential Information Memorandum packages sealed and ready for delivery by—

7:45 a.m.

The firm was growing.

Ballon forgot today was the start date for four new colleagues.

"Record year," Goldman kept hammering at their weekly staff meetings.

Record year equals record bonuses, the bullpenners all discussed.

Smoke was all but rising off of Ballon's keyboard as he updated the acquirer tracking sheet at the precise moment that Goldman was taking around the new managing director, who was tall with a slightly rosy complexion, gorgeous smile, and standard-issue Hermes tie that rose and fell with his paunch as he spoke.

It took Goldman a couple calls into Bale's cubicle to break his concentration:

"Sorry, Mr. Goldman, working away here," Bale said.

"This is Paul Schmidt, the new managing director. He will be growing our Hotel, Restaurant, and Recreation vertical. He joins us from Lazard."

Ballon got up and shook his hand, saying something like "Welcome to... " and awkwardly trailing off, being unable to come up with anything witty or non-perverse to say. Within a couple seconds Ballon was back at his Tracking Sheet. Presumably, Goldman took Schmidt around to meet whomever else was in the office. Ballon didn't know. It was as if the side streets, driveways, and byways of his mind had been closed and a great main interstate had been opened devoted exclusively to Tracking Sheets.

In another hour, he had gathered a stack of FedEx envelopes so high that the column reached over the top of the cubicle. It took a well-placed stress ball rocket released from the hands of Fredericks to derail Ballon's momentum.

"Asshole," Ballon muttered.

"Come on, little guy, cheer up. It's Friday. Big night tonight for us," Fredericks said, now at his desk.

"What's going on?" Bale said.

"Did you forget? It's Boxing Night, little fella. The one Friday we are guaranteed to get outta here at 5 p.m.," Fredericks said, referring to an amateur boxing match arranged by the Union League Club. "Because the event starts at 6. Scotch, steak, and cigars. Even Escher will allow himself a drink or two. The elephant pussy."

Ballon didn't look up.

"What is it with you, Balo? You're in here earlier than usual but your sprightly demeanor is betrayed by the smell of liquor and pussy and self-loathing. Your whole cube is inundated."

The word "liquor" summoned McAllister who was eating only one half of a bagel toasted with a thin layer of cream cheese. This caused Fredericks temporarily to forget Bale existed.

"Will you put a reasonable amount of cream cheese on that thing next time, McAllister, youuu fucking pussy?"

McAllister produced a noiseless, wide-mouthed laugh.

"Anyway, I was just noticing that the above-average productivity in this cubicle does not correspond with the stench of alcohol and pussy — or is it fear? — coming from every pore of the little guy's body."

"Yeah, dude, you reek," McAllister said.

"Fuck. Do you think Goldman noticed?"

"Yes," Fredericks said, rolling his eyes.

"Do you think Schiltz noticed?" Ballon said with panic in his voice.

"Yes," Fredericks said, "and the man's name is *Schmidt*. Might want to jot that down somewhere."

"Shit."

"We are not leaving without an explanation."

"I went out last night."

"Naww," McAllister said.

"Had a date. Went well. Ended."

"That shirt is new," McAllister said.

"Her ol' man's."

McAllister roared so excitedly that bagel-spittle

flew from his mouth.

Bale filled them in on some of the details, reserving the risqué ones for after hours. Toward the end, he implied his productivity was from some inversely proportional manifestation of "repentance" for destroying an invaluable Spanish artifact, which seemed to satisfy both of them, and they exited with Fredericks trying to knock the thinly adorned bagel out of McAllister's hands.

Ballon paused. *Would he actually be able to keep up today's ethic for a decade or more?*

These thoughts might have—on a normal day— caused a few hiccups in his mental focus. But today? Well, he was *Pigouing* today.

9 a.m.

Sherry led the newest V.P. through the bullpen. The man had affixed his eyes at her curves so obviously and unwaveringly even McAllister and Fredericks shared looks of embarrassment.

Fredericks broke the man's stare by offering premature introductions, rapid-fire, to prevent Sherry turning around to introduce him and him slamming into her like a drooling corporate zombie.

The V.P.'s name was Archibald Thomas.

Everything was unctuous about Archie, starting with slicked-back hair that looked like a Lucite helmet. A bulky caloric formless blob with peg legs and a chest that heaved even when he was standing still.

Their reservation at Petterino's was set for 1 p.m. and, as they crossed Daley Plaza, Archibald Thomas was telling horrifying personal anecdotes about his fondness for L'Occitane hand cream and post-meal sex.

"So I get my AmEx bill this month and I am like 'Honey, you got a minute to go over this?' I mean, I go out to dinner a couple nights a week and I have drinks with friends a couple nights a week but I get my bill for one month and it is well over fifteen thousand dollars. That's one credit card. So I'm like, 'Honey, why is the bill so high this month?' And she's like, 'Well, I haven't done much shopping this month. Just the usual grocery store, Pilates, book club-type stuff, so it must be yours.' So I say 'Alright' and I print the statement. We're talking 20 pages. And I go through and I highlight all of my charges and bring it back to her for review—"

This is how far our species has come. Down from the trees, through swamps and tundra and ocean, pestilence and famine and world wars ... to hand cream and itemized credit card statements.

2:09 p.m.

After lunch, back in the bullpen, the mystery of Bale's physical condition took a strange twist.

Bale, for an unknown reason felt as though he had just finished running a marathon. He felt lethargic and faded, depressed and even a touch hungry, remembering that he only had one bite of his turkey club at lunch. He hadn't eaten a full meal in over twelve hours but was only beginning to feel hunger pangs and hadn't smoked a cigarette all day.

He must be terminally ill.

He couldn't keep his eyes open, let along stare at the computer screen. His fingers ached for the first time and he suddenly became concerned with several other previously under-the-radar problems, such as weekend plans, paying his rent and health club dues, and did he make reservations for the family's dinner tonight at Avec? He needed an espresso-spiked coffee.

Bale suddenly remembered.

He was standing on Mara Shiffman's parent's balcony, with his back toward the French doors, dragging on his cigarette stub. The fading smoke met Mara's face when she returned to him, wearing a devilish grin. That was all she wore.

She held a glass of water and two large pills.

"It's like cocaine, but legal," she said, though Bale could not possibly hear that as he looked over her glabrous body. She held the pill aloft for him, like a priestess offering him Christ's body.

Studying medical websites, he identified that it was a 30 mg capsule of Adderall XR, an extended-release dose of amphetamines.

He also noted a warning:

AMPHETAMINES HAVE A HIGH POTENTIAL FOR ABUSE. PARTICULAR ATTENTION SHOULD BE PAID TO THE POSSIBILITY OF SUBJECTS OBTAINING AM-

PHETAMINES FOR NON-THERAPEUTIC USE OR DIS-
TRIBUTION TO OTHERS AND THE DRUGS SHOULD
BE PRESCRIBED OR DISPENSED SPARINGLY.

And:

MISUSE OF AMPHETAMINE MAY CAUSE SUDDEN
DEATH AND SERIOUS CARDIOVASCULARLY-ADVERSE
EVENTS.

Then he texted Mara.

"Great time last night. Let's do it again soon.
Those pills we took are fantastic. Can I buy a bunch of
them from you?"

He thought about, and deleted, the last two sentences, and sent the text.

All in good time.

Post-redeye, Bale's prospects were on the uptick.
Work was minimal because of his super-human a.m.
push. A notification from Outlook popped up on his
screen: Meeting with Escher, 3:30 p.m.

3:01 p.m.

The *Chicago Tribune* reported a hostage situation
at Ogilvie train station on Madison Avenue, where Fredericks caught his train to the suburbs. Bale went to in-
form him.

"Fredericks. Hostage situation. Madman with
guns at Ogilvie."

Fredericks didn't even nod his head: "Yeaaaah

the trains are all backed up."

"There is a man slaying people in the train station. I think there are a couple dead already. He's holding others hostage inside an emptied-out Corner Bakery."

"Right, yes, I saw," Fredericks said.

"Aren't you bothered by this?"

Fredericks stopped typing. He made a quarter turn so Bale could see his pockmarked cheek twitching.

"There is always some wacko or fundamentalist shooting or blowing something up," he said. "The question is, how will it affect me?"

"In a sense of course that has to be the most basic initial reaction to violence but don't you care that people are dying?"

"People I never met?"

"Yes."

"Fuck man. No, I don't. I'd prefer they didn't, but I can't control anything in life except my own actions. I just try to put my head down and get on with it."

He swiveled around in his chair to face Bale.

"Look, my dad was a road construction worker. Paved roads and flagged cars all around Dubuque. One day, a maniac driver mowed down his entire work crew on Route 20. He was the only one that survived. Was away on break, finishing a cigarette. Afterward, he didn't donate blood or move to an ashram in India or even change jobs. He walked in the front door, sat down at dinner, and said, "Meatloaf again, Martha?"

Bale sighed and walked off for his Escher meeting.

3:31 p.m.

Escher was wrapping up a conversation with the new managing director, Schmidt, and the new V.P., Archibald Thomas, who was already rattling off pitch-worthy companies with revenues over one hundred million dollars in his vertical. And it was good timing, Paul Schmidt said, that Bale was present because he wanted to compile an exhaustive list of companies in that space by Monday.

Really nice thing, Schmidt-head, giving an analyst five hours of weekend work your first fucking day on the job, Bale thought. *I bet Archibald can rattle off enough companies in the Hotel, Restaurant, and Recreation Industries simply by listing the establishments he has been thrown out of in the last year alone.*

"Absolutely, Mr. Schmidt. You'll have it Monday morning."

They all nodded with satisfaction.

Sherry walked by as the meeting ended and Thomas left, flagging her down—something about needing help setting up his voicemail. Bale was unsuccessful in trying not to roll his eyes.

"Take a seat, Bale," Escher said. "Thanks."

Bale did.

"How are things going?"

"Fine. You?"

"Listen. I have to talk to you about something.

First, you're working very hard and we all appreciate it. So, thank you for that. You can see that we are growing around here and heading in a direction that I think will position us as one of the top middle-market banks in the United States. There are a couple things that I want to make you aware of as areas of improvement. Personally, I think you are a nice guy. But lately your attitude, in a couple of our dealings, has been, well, not so amiable. I understand that there is a lot of pressure on you guys and you work very hard. But keep in mind that there is a certain level of professional courtesy that you are obligated to pay to your supervisors. Be that Martin or Jim or myself."

"OK," Bale said. "I am sorry about that."

Ballon returned to his desk. Despite loathing Escher, he knew the man's orders had to be followed. A possible $85,000 bonus depended on it. He checked his phone. He had a text from Mara who said she wanted to have drinks Saturday night. He thought about Escher's talk with him and decided there were three things that would help him immediately:

1) A cigarette
2) Sex
3) Five drinks
4) A steady intake of Adderal XR

He responded "perfect" to Mara's invitation and made a reservation.

While the entire office was walking in a pack to the Union League Club, Bale was pulling logos from websites and pasting them to each company profile he had created.

Ballon only had thirty-eight more to pull when the Hurricane swaggered to his cube and draped his arms Christ-like across its entrance.

"You realize it is fight night, don't you?"

Ballon took a second or two, because he was shocked by the Hurricane's wardrobe, which consisted of chest waders, thick flannel shirt, and fly-pierced hat.

Seeing the waders reminded Bale of the worn pair his father kept hanging from a nail inside the garage at the Michigan house, and Bruce tinkering with boxes of steelhead flies and fishing lines, organizing his pack for their first trip to the river more than a decade earlier. Looking back on the doting pleasure clear on Bruce's face as he held Bale's hand over the cork handle teaching him to cast, or his father hollering with pride a month later when Bale cradled his first steelhead in the slack water near their favorite hole, seemed like scenes from an old foreign movie.

"Yeah, I, uh, just wanted to get this rolling before the weekend."

"Good. Want to ride with me?"

"Yes, thanks." Ballon went in his desk drawer and removed a rolled-up tie and threaded it through his collar. He saved the Excel work and grabbed his wallet and keys and followed the Hurricane to his office.

Bale leaned against the wall as the Hurricane grabbed a hanging, plastic-covered suit ensemble and a little leather tote bag containing a change of underwear, necktie, black socks, and rolled black belt. His fishing rod was in its case next to the wall.

"You need a minute to change?"

"I'll shower and change there."

"Will they let you?"

"I'm on the board."

"Ah."

The massive oak-framed room at the Union League Club of Chicago had been transformed into a grotesque masculine fantasy, from the makeshift canvas boxing ring dribbled with talcum powder and blood to the woman in a bikini and heels toting a ROUND 7 sign.

Men scratched steak knives against porcelain plates atop gravy-stained linen, their bellies heaped with cigar ash. Those not gorging themselves were snickering, cursing, and spewing punch lines while swapping cigars from mouth to hand.

At one point a man fell off his chair in an alcoholic daze.

Bale was sitting in the first quarter of the table, Fredericks to his left, Rothkauf on the right, McAllister in front, and the new intern adjacent. The ring was about twenty feet away—just far enough from the flying sweat and blood and occasional mouth guard.

Ballon watched carefully as a cutman sliced a

bloated bump on the fighter's face. The pugilist hardly winced. The blood drained and the assistant trainer squirted water into his mouth. Boxers and writers are the only humans who sacrifice literally everything to entertain.

8:37 p.m.

Bale was four drinks deep by the time he pried himself from the club. He sucked down a quick cigarette before hailing a cab.

"Avec. Randolph. Past 94."

He listened to the city, the breeze poured against him through the open window like salt water. The moon lounged in the vermillion sky. There were clots of traffic as Chicago ramped up for Friday night.

These dinners with his family used to be weekly, when he first started at the bank, then fortnightly, then monthly. This evening marked more than three months since he had to look his father squarely in the eyes.

But what was there to say to his family at this *pro forma* dinner? He thought of the endless stream of minor achievements of his job, the pleasureless tasks he did in exchange for heaps of money and the promise of a grand pay-off still weeks away.

Perhaps there was some news item he could use to trigger the exchange of lightly informed opinions in between courses?

Suddenly he felt shabby in his day-rotten clothing. His mind swirled from the booze, confused dispassion, and Sisyphean emptiness.

He felt that the city's hot oxygen was tainted and breathed nervously. He unlocked his iPhone and scrolled hoping for a message. Anything *new*. But there was nothing. And it made him feel isolated and sad.

As they moved through intersections and the bridge over I-94, he imagined the dinner unfolding as it already had a million times.

I'll get there and Dad'll say you're late and complain about coming all the way downtown in rush hour traffic and then he'll just sit stoically and slurp his soup and ask backhanded and contemptible questions about my lifestyle. And Mom'll try and elevate the discussion to the city's response to police brutality, and Dad'll make awful comments about "low-lifes" and "protecting business owners."

And while Mom shoos his opinions away like a hornet swarm, I'll try to eliminate silence from our table with pretend-interest questions. But there is only one topic Dad'll want to discuss: "How's work?"

Or maybe he'll ask me about my plan to take the GMAT. He is very fucking epically concerned about my plans regarding that test.

Your scores are valid for three years, he'll say, and suggest I take the test while my college exam-taking skills are still fresh; and tell me again about his best friend Blake Schepp at Credit Suisse who makes "like 20 mil' a year."

And when it gets to be too much, he'll start getting *the feeling*—a vague perception so small he isn't sure that it is even there—just a microscopic inkling that I think I am better than him, that I can see through him and see that above all he is a cynical bastard.

He will be examining, judging this possibility and wondering if I am subtly communicating to him in the sly, bellicose way only kin truly can.

When the bill comes I will—because I will be drunk as always and trying to show him how great I am doing professionally—reach for my wallet and wag my finger "no" and this'll make him very proud, because his son, at the age of twenty-two, is fighting through the world on his own and able to make such a powerful American gesture of greatness.

And, as the waiter goes to swipe my Visa, I will remember that I am supposed to comment on the importance of accumulating awards points so that I can upgrade to First Class during a future trip to Vail or Aspen for a winter holiday.

AT THE LAKE HOUSE

Michigan: Saturday, November 2019

Late afternoon.

"—everyone talks about Hemingway and his hunting and fishing and masculinity and whatnot but Lord Byron kept a fucking *bear* in his room at Cambridge," Sutton was saying as he shoved yet another log into the stove in the freestanding sauna behind the Ratcliffe lakeside mansion.

Sutton and Bale had been together for 24 hours, hiding out since Bale fled the city after the office blowup.

"It's not like he lived in a fucking zoo — this was a dorm room, not much bigger than ours was," Sutton said. "Wilde kept *blue china* at Oxford."

Sutton closed the stove door, latched it, and sprayed water at the stove, which hissed and moaned and eructed a huge plume of steam.

Bale watched the thermostat climb and rubbed the sweat from his eyes. His lungs burned. His finger skin rippled.

Sutton, performing a series of stretches that lacked enough effort to achieve anything, said, "So Byron—George Gordon Noel Byron—was basically a rock star by twenty-eight, Balfour. Twenty-eight. Legions of female followers, independently wealthy, as a *poet.* I want you to think about that."

Sutton picked up the water bottle and blasted the iron, which unleashed a vicious belch of scorching steam. They both started coughing uncontrollably.

"Did you know he slept with Mary Shelley's step-sister?" Sutton said. He started thumping his chest with his fist and hacking. "Had a kid, in fact he had several children, out of wedlock."

Bale crossed his legs and bridge-gapped them with an old *New York Times* puzzle he tore free from a stack of kindling.

"Who was the star of *Ninotchka*?" Bale said.

"Byron also," Sutton said, but was cut off by the crossword puzzle question. "How many letters?"

"Five."

Sutton took long deep breaths, and then glacially slouched toward his toes.

"He got a boat, as I was saying, Byron got a boat, planned to arm it with mercenaries and sail to Greece during their war of independence to fight the Ottomans—"

"Really?"

"Yeah, man. Can you imagine? This aristocratic

manic-depressive philandering literary sex maniac sailed to fucking Greece in a private war ship. I mean, imagine *Frost* doing that."

"Raymond Carver couldn't even sail his own bathtub," Bale said.

Sutton laugh-choked, then began trying to wedge the second of two enormous logs into the stove's orifice. Flames leapt out of the hole, singeing his fingers. He took the poker and crammed them in and forced the door closed.

"I think we are good as far as heat goes, Sutts."

"One more good spray though."

"Sutts."

"Just one abbreviated one."

"Sutton, no."

He took the bottle and vigorously sprayed a thick jet of water up and down the stove's top and its stack, which moaned and hissed and popped for several seconds and filled the sauna with scalding steam.

They coughed and moaned and grimaced.

"Awgh," Bale said, hunching over.

"This is helping you," Sutton said. "Your real battle is mental, not physical."

Sutton leaned down and rested his palms above his knees.

"How'd Byron do in battle?" Bale asked.

"That's not the point but he died on the boat before it even set sail, poor bastard. Fever of some sort."

"A fever?"

"Well, they relentlessly bloodletted him."

Bale's breath pushed steam.

"Do you understand what I am saying to you, B.R.?" Sutton said.

"I think so. Partially."

"'Our life exhales, a little breath, love, wine, ambition, fame, fighting, devotion, dust—perhaps a name,'" Sutton said. "That is what Bryon wrote."

Bale stared for several minutes at the flames in the stove window.

"Garbo?" Sutton said.

"What?"

"Your crossword question. G-a-r-b-o. Swede-American actress."

"Ah, nice one," Bale said, filling in the letters. "What should we do today?"

"Friday we drank and fished," Sutton said. "It's Saturday. Why don't we drink and fish?"

Bale smiled.

"You really should have some water," Bale said, holding the water bottle out for Sutton.

"'I don't drink water. Fish fuck in it. W. C. Fields.'"

They laughed, then gagged and choked.

"We could try the north fork for steelhead," Bale said.

"It looks pretty nasty out there man, with the wind and rain," Sutton said.

"Just imagine hooking into a ten-pound buck."

"Cold too."

"What would *Byron* do?" Bale said.

"That is the best point you possibly could have made," Sutton said, seeing his message to his friend was sinking in.

"We'll have to go north an hour and a half," Bale started saying, but he was interrupted by the sound of a car door slamming shut, which was rare in the forested property with no other homes or people for thirty acres.

"Who the fuck is that?" Bale said.

Bale wrapped the towel around his waist and walked out of the sauna into the biting fall air.

Slivers of sunlight clawed through the forest canopy. He smelt the vaginal odor of wet mulch. A red fox bounded over a tractor path.

Dizzy from the sauna heat and near continuous drinking, he moved carefully a few paces towards the noise. His eyes squinted down along the shallow grade to the gravel roundabout, past a few trees, where he saw his father's silver Mercedes and the outline of two adults shouldering weekend-sized bags walking up the pathway to the house.

"Bale?! Honey, is that you?!" his mother said.

"What are you doing here!?" his father called, his voice expressing equal measures of surprise and concern. "When did you get here?"

Bale tried to look composed.

"Oh, just a couple hours ago," he lied.

Bruce's long strides overtook the incline leading to the house.

"You ain't got a broad in there, do ya?" Bruce called out.

"You should've called us," Ruth yelled, trailing behind him.

"We tried your phone but it went straight to voicemail," Bruce said.

"Oh, I turned it off—wanted some peace out here," Bale said.

"So Fredericks let you off the hook this weekend?"

"Yeah, well—"

"Honey, what happened to your eye!?" Ruth said.

"It's a long story," Bale said. He began fumbling for words before Sutton emerged from the sauna.

"Greetings, Ratcliffe family!" Sutton yelled.

"Ah, hey there, Sutton," Bruce yelled.

With Bruce and Ruth momentarily tied up talking to him, Bale rushed into the house and un-clogged and stashed two ashtrays, threw out the empty bottle of whiskey, rounded up a herd of empty glasses and stained plates and stacked up an explosion of Sutton's magazines and newspapers and dog-eared books. He flipped on a ceiling fan and popped open a window for a couple minutes of fresh airflow.

"It smells like a French whore house," Bruce said, as he crossed into the kitchen. Ruth whispered through her freshly manicured fingers: "I can't stay here like this."

Bruce closed his eyes. Exhaled. "Your mother and I are going to go into town for a drink and to pick up groceries. Have this place cleaned up by the time I get back."

It was nearly 7:20 p.m. when Ruth's singing laughter could be heard in the vestibule.

"Well, this *is* much better," Ruth said, placing two heaping bags of groceries on the kitchen counter. She rolled her eyes at the boys, who were cleanly shaved and adorned in fresh clothing.

"You two," Ruth said, smiling and shaking her head. She hugged Sutton and then Bale, pausing afterward to gently touch the strap of his eye patch and give him a look of loving pity.

"We picked up a nice roast at the market. We'll have a salad with it—it's *so good* to get out of the city," Ruth said, taking a head of lettuce from a brown bag.

"How wonderful to find you both here."

"Is there anything we can do to help prepare for dinner, Ruth?" Sutton said.

"I would like you to pour me a glass of red wine and I would like my long-lost son to tell me about his life."

Sutton set about the wine. Ballon set about the fiction.

THE BANK

Chicago: August–November 2019

9:14 a.m.

Saturday morning. Mid-August. Ballon's apartment. The sound of a jackhammer assaulting concrete poured through Ballon's east-facing bedroom, shocking him awake.

His head pounded like the hammer and he found it difficult to move without upsetting the gravid barrels of alcohol and meat sloshing in the hold of his stomach.

This is very bad, he thought, attempting to lift his head.

He had grown accustomed to early morning trauma/drama and had worked out a cure for the common hangover. Such a cure had eluded the best minds in science for centuries and he felt he should be given a Nobel Prize.

It was a poorly defined problem, however. Merriam-Webster said a hangover was "disagreeable physical effects (headache and nausea) from heavy consumption of alcohol or drugs."

But "disagreeable" is like a hangnail, a dour co-worker. This morning was closer to intercranial violence.

It was that plus withdrawal and an intangible/unnameable quality he called *pre-hepatic comatic paralysis (P-HCP)*, cutely, an application derived from the Glasgow Coma Scale which assesses the severity of a brain injury on a scale from three to fifteen, with three being the lowest chance of recovery.

Based on his symptoms, his P-HCP rating would be around 6.5.

He began his recovery:

1) *Take painkiller*

He went to the bathroom and sucked down a Percocet.

2) *Smoke cigarette*

3) *Coffee*

Ballon inserted a little plastic single-serve capsule and pushed a back-lit BREW button. Hot coffee appeared in in the receiving terminal a minute later. The quality of the coffee itself was unimportant compared to its speed.

4) *Smoke another cigarette*

5) *Take two huge rips of marijuana*

6-7-8) *Shit. Shower. And Shave.*

Ballon turned the shower dial to its hottest setting. While the bathroom steamed up, Ballon sat on the toilet with his sweaty palms pressed to his thumping forehead and his lungs like soggy sponges, and emptied his bowels in agony.

In the shower, he compulsively washed every inch of his body, moaning as the scalding water caused painful pleasure. He rubbed a thick, lilac-scented towel, over his body and loins and dried his hair. His eyes were sallow and blood shot. He saw a muted shadow of beard and decided, frivolously, to leave it until Monday morning.

He dressed in beige shorts, suede slip-ons, and a gray polo.

Someone knocked on the door. Bale opened it and found Sutton, holding Bale's *Tribune*, which Bale had subscribed to in print because holding its pages reminded him of London and his short period of joy working at the newspaper.

Now it depressed him to see the hulking mass of pages stuffed in its white plastic, a forgotten indulgence, a beckoning child he didn't have time for. An emblem of his dream deferred. He missed writing so badly that a random story by Mary Wisniewski on a pigeon shit plague nearly brought him to tears.

He tossed the paper in the recycling.

11:45 a.m.

Step #9 was a lavish brunch and step #10 was to drink numerous nerve-numbing alcoholic concoctions.

At an elegant patio off Lincoln Avenue, Bale and Sutton ordered steak and eggs, two Bloody Marys, two coffees and a pitcher of ice water. Sutton, who despised small talk, was surprised by how little Bale had to say— not a word on politics, economics, literature, theater, art, new explorations or romance—and finally said: "How is work?"

"*Tough* man.

"I see."

"Hours piling up."

"Brutal."

Sutton spoke for a while about law school and joining a team of students working to overturn a man's wrongful murder conviction.

The silliness of Bale's work made it barely worth mentioning. They fell silent again.

"What'd you do last night?" Bale said.

"Had dinner with my parents."

"Nice. How was it?"

"Good, good. Went to Halligan afterward. Texted you."

The waitress reappeared with the drinks.

He had done it, achieved through chemical and caloric consumption a stately numbness of mind and body.

Until the food arrived, Ballon watched through his sunglasses the leaves torn free by the wind spin down into the gutter.

. . . . .

11:30 a.m.

Monday morning. Late-August.

Chicago was, as the Hurricane put it, "hotter than two squirrels fucking in a wool sock."

Bale was knackered. Analysts can't sleep properly on Sunday nights. You cannot drink yourself into an early-morning coma both weekend nights and expect to fall asleep at 10:30 p.m. on Sunday. He tossed until 4 a.m.

So he was all but chugging his espresso-injected coffee when the new managing director Paul Schmidt came to his desk and chucked five thick pitch books into the cubicle which knocked a calculator and pens and a refinancing deal's tombstone on the floor.

"Jesus!" was what Bale said.

"Did you even look at these before you gave them to me?"

"Yeah, I—"

"Shut up. *Shut up*," Schmidt strived to say quietly. "Pick any one of them and open to the profiles. Now."

Ballon scooped up one of the books at his feet and flipped through to the profiles.

"Do you see anything missing?"

Bale turned page by page.

"DO YOU SEE ANYTHING MISSING?"

Bale got to the section where the names, portraits and masturbatory bios were displayed.

"Uh-hum, yes," Ballon said quietly. "Your profile."

"MY profile. *Mine.*"

"Yes."

"Do you realize that I was sitting in front of the Board of Fucking Directors at Bell Point and the CFO asked if there was information about the bankers who would work on the deal, and I said, 'Of course there is, all of the bankers who would form your Deal Team are profiled in the back' and told him the page number to flip to, not in a million years considering even the slightest possibility that *my* profile, as the M.D. who would *lead* the deal, would not be there!"

Schmidt went on for quite a while like this, listing other issues.

"This is *crazy*," Schmidt said. "You are better than this. Get it together."

He walked off.

Ballon spun back around and stared blankly at his screen.

He tried to figure out what was wrong. The work wasn't complex or particularly intellectually difficult. Was the paycheck failing to offset his apathy toward stupid work? Was he sabotaging himself to indirectly get back at his father? Was he simply losing his mind?

He started cleaning up the mess.

2:30 p.m.

There was an email from Sherry.

"B. R.—sorry to hear about the mistake. I can't believe what an asshole Schmidt is. Hang in there :)"

"Dude, she totally wants to fuck you," McAllister said, reading over Bale's shoulder.

Bale jumped.

"You fucking startled me dude."

"You've been a bit punchy all morning. But who wouldn't be after that assault?"

"Thanks."

"Wait," McAllister said. "Did you *already* fuck her?"

"No, man."

"Dude, tell me the truth."

"No, I did not. I *would* not."

"That's right, dude," McAllister said. "You don't shit where you eat."

"Yeah."

"But she totally wants to fuck you."

. . . . .

The next day. 9:23 a.m.

Ballon was able to time the fading hold of Adderall XR with rapid intake of caffeine so that the transfer from drug to drug was tolerably flawless. Still there were severe drawbacks that came with the loss of bursting amphetamine capsules to his cranial receptors: depression, exhaustion and the insatiable need to itch his feet and an unstoppable underarm sweat release.

Although his body was used to the transition, he needed to facilitate it with 1,200 reps with a stress ball and some ten glasses of water throughout the day to quell the constant feeling of terror and dehydration (about which he planned to ask the head of toxicology at Rush University Medical Center during their next video interface). This morning, because the filtration tank in the kitchen had to be changed—and he wasn't going to lower himself to drinking fucking tap water—jitters, shakes, and precursory anxiety gripped his central nervous system.

The simple act of Fredericks bouncing a tennis ball into his cubicle in a smooth inverted parabola nearly sent Ratcliffe crashing to the floor.

"Christ, son, a little stressed today?"

"This week has been particularly bad."

"Hmmmm. Let's get a shoeshine. That'll set you right. On me."

"Give me twenty?"

"Yep."

Fredericks went to pay a visit to Rothkauf (who was not at his desk).

"Take note," Fredericks said to the whole bullpen, sputtering with laughter, "it is 9:24 a.m. on Wednesday morning and J. B. Rothkauf is nowhere to be found."

Ballon got up and went to Rothkauf's desk and

began to embed several settings into his computer that would take Rothkauf the better part of an hour to undue: Bale reversed his mouse button settings, switched the default back-room printer to Escher's personal one, and changed Rothkauf's login password—and logged out.

Bale was back at his desk brooding over his ailing health when Escher stopped by holding—crushing, really—a Confidential Information Memorandum.

Escher, physically suppressing rage, started with a harshly whispered question.

"When you bind a book, do you go page by page through them to check for problems?"

"Yes. Of course."

An accurate answer would've been: *Yes, I always do. Except, however, last night, because I had a cataclysmic fucking headache and went page by page through the first ten books but then gradually tapered off my thoroughness on books eleven through fifteen.*

"On page *sixty-one* of this book, in the *middle* of the Financial Overview Section for the Praxis deal that you sent to Jim Caddup at Blue Sky Acquisitions, there is a *confidential* Letter of Intent—*from another deal*—bound *into* it."

Escher looked like he might have a cardiac episode.

Bale apologized profusely.

"This is a monumental fuck up," Escher said. He walked away in a stunned, zombie-like manner.

"Week getting worse?" Fredericks said, back at Ballon's cubicle.

"Yeah."

"Fucked up something else?"

"Yeah."

"Ready for that shine?"

"Yeah."

. . . . .

Mid-September. The office of Dr. David Q. Oglethorpe, *Head of Toxicology*, Rush University Medical System.

Ballon cringed every time he shifted his naked body on the wax paper lining of the examination table. He was scrolling through his iPhone from a horizontal position as the doctor pushed on various points of his belly.

"How long since your last physical?"

"About a year."

"How is your health generally?"

"Isn't that what I am here to find out?"

"Stomach feels normal. Good. Sit up."

He placed the cold stethoscope along points of Bale's chest and upper back, telling him to breathe deeply.

"Your breathing is labored," The doctor said before peering deeply into Bale's nostril. "How do you feel at different points of the day?"

Bale lowered his iPhone.

"I still have that daytime sweating problem that

we discussed, doctor. It isn't like, *pouring*, all over my body. It's just my underarms. But it is usually constant. I have tried the most expensive antiperspirants, which have not fixed the problem, so I basically just go to the bathroom, undo my shirt, and use paper towels, like eight times a day."

"OK. Anything else?"

"Well, I read online about botox shots for your arm pits, is that an option?"

"I mean, anything *else*? Any general health concerns?"

"I get chest pains."

Oglethorpe cleared his throat.

"Stand up," he said. He asked Ballon to do a squatting action, like one does with a free-weight bar across the shoulders. Oglethorpe put his stethoscope to Bale's chest and squatted with him, the two in coordination, completing three sets.

"OK. Good." He scribbled some notes.

"How old are you?" Oglethorpe asked.

"Twenty-three."

"Tell me Bale, do you feel like you have a lot of really bad, day-to-day," he cringed and made a claw out of his left hand, "stress?"

"Yes."

"Do you ever feel overwhelmed by it?"

"Yes."

"Tell me about your lifestyle. Would you say that you work a lot?"

"Ninety hours a week, on average."

The doctor blinked rapidly.

"How about your sleep pattern? Do you feel well rested? Like, when you wake up in the morning?"

"Well-rested?"

"Your caffeine intake?"

"Constant."

"And your diet? How many meals would you say you eat out at restaurants each week?"

"I eat all meals out every day."

The doctor scribbled.

"Do you smoke?"

"Aggressively."

"How many packs a week?"

"Uh, two packs during the week. One pack on each of the weekend days. I smoke more when I drink."

"And how often do you drink?"

"Socially?"

"Drinking should always be social. How many drinks would you say you have a week?"

"I don't know. Thirty-five?"

"Thirty-five?!" the doctor aped, which sounded to Bale as if he was seeking to verify the statement rather than expressing shock over the quantity.

"I dunno, forty?"

"Forty?! OK, I have one word for you: *moderation.* You need to rethink your lifestyle, everything from your drinking and smoking to the amount of caffeine you are consuming. You are putting your body through a lot."

As he was leaving the office, an administrative assistant tracked him down holding the largest possible coffee Starbucks sells.

"Sir," she said to Bale, "you left this in the waiting room."

· · · · ·

September 27, 2019. Friday night.

6:35 p.m.

On the curb outside Stocks and Blondes on Wells and Washington, over the course of two cigarettes, the following phone conversation took place.

"Hey, Katzman."

"Ratcliffe you Christ-killer motherfucker! How's it going man?"

"Good. You?"

"I am going to pick up some coke.

"Fine. Fine. Listen, I just got my prorated bonus, we need to talk."

"Prorated bonus, what's that?"

"Like a mid-year-review-based installment. My bonus was too low. My review was above average despite a couple black spots, but it's been a banner year at the firm, by all measures.

"You're in middle-market banking, baby. Gotta-go bulge-bracket."

"New York?"

"I'd recommend it. It'll be more hours but a ton more money. I bet I can get you in here at JPMorgan. They love me here. It would be amazing to work together."

"Thanks man."

"Listen, before you go, I have to tell you something. You are not going to like it. I saw Meta while I was Jdating."

"Where?

"At a restaurant in Midtown."

"What'd she say?"

"Nothing."

"Nothing? I thought you said you saw her at a restaurant?"

"Correct. I *saw* her. Didn't speak to her."

"How's she look?"

"Incredible."

"*Fantastic.*"

"These are facts. She had a nice profile in the *Times* ahead of her upcoming movie."

"Great."

"What is your status? You guys talking, still have feelings or what?"

"I have to go."

Back inside the bar, McAllister had lined the table with beer-backed whisky shots.

"Getting after it, huh?" Bale said.

McAllister looked at him, lifted a whisky and

poured it down his throat. Bale quickly did the same.

"Goldman offered me a full-time associate job after I graduate from Chicago. Told me on our flight back from Atlanta that he thinks I have it in me to be a vice president within 4 years."

"Dude, that's amazing!" Bale said.

"I'd make half a mil' a year and I wouldn't be thirty-two."

"I am so happy for you, man!"

"It was the single greatest moment of my life," McAllister said. "I just felt *big*, you know? Hurrying home from O'Hare to tell Stephanie, I just couldn't wait to tell her."

His eyes watered.

"But when I got to the apartment, she was gone. Everything of hers was gone. I called her and she said she was at her brother's place in Ann Arbor and that she was tired of everything and she wished it could have worked out and that she loved me but she was just tired of waiting. She used that word a lot—tired tired tired—I asked her why she was giving up and I begged her to explain and how could she just *leave* like that with no explanation, you know? And I'll never forget what she said as long as I live: 'The fact that you would even ask me that convinces me of how right I was to leave.'"

McAllister stared at the bubbles rising in his pint.

"I guess she mentioned some things over the past few months but... " he said. He suddenly dropped his face into his palms and sobbed, his shoulders jumping up and down. "She will not take my calls. I wanted to just tell her... what I had done... it was for us... the future it would have given us."

Bale pulled McAllister by the shoulder and hugged him.

Bale thought about what to say. *Work will get easier to manage. You're better off without her. She'll come around.* All lies.

"I am so sorry, man," was all he could muster.

10:23 p.m.

Bale popped awake on a couch in a foreign apartment, a number of hours later, dripping sweat in the darkness.

The noise of a shower running in the bathroom a few paces away signaled another human presence. In front on him, on a wobbly IKEA coffee table, was a bottle of Jim Beam, empty beer cans, freshly laid rails of unsucked cocaine, and hookah tentacles next to a cannabis-stuffed Ziploc.

Suddenly, he felt blood dripping down his back and handcuffs fastened from his wrist to one of the table's rickety legs.

He heard the most beautiful voice he had ever heard in person twisting off the shower walls. Some jazz music also came out of a speaker on the room's corner table, which also held a pile of poetry and fiction, all of which Ballon had been intimately familiar with in college and London, but whose words he could only vaguely recall now.

A girl emerged from the bathroom savaging her hair with a towel and muttering a collection of phrases that sounded possibly Russian.

Her tattooed chest brought back to him flashes of the beating she delivered on him, riding his poor phallus and digging her nails into his back until she came and she pulled the soggy condom off him and dropped it in the trash can and went for a shower.

He remembered now that she was a woman of feisty intellect whom he had met when he was helping McAllister, who was blinding drunk, out of a cab at his apartment building. She had laughed at the disabled pair and he told her, "You should see the other guy," and they had a good laugh and then a cigarette and then drinks at the Old Town Ale House.

She returned to the bathroom and slammed the door. He could make out parts of her language. It was possibly actually Croatian. Doroteja, was her name.

With her hidden away, he yanked his cuffed hand until the table's leg cracked off, pulled on his clothes and shoes, clawed for his wallet, keys, cigarettes, and phone and careened toward the door.

But as he passed a hall mirror, he noticed that the back of his shirt had several diagonal blood stains. He thought about going to the hospital.

He unlocked the door bolt with extreme caution, and when it came free with a little click, he tiptoed out the door, closed it, and took off limping down the corridor.

But he stopped midway and ran back to the door and tucked his business card under the door frame. It wasn't a *completely* bad evening, all in all.

After a halting ride in a deficient elevator, he was chased by the nighttime doorman for some unknown alleged offense and was sprinting at full speed down the street with his only thought being how shockingly good Allen Edmonds shoes hold up during urban flee-running.

He paused after rounding onto Sheffield from Fullerton, heaving and gasping, and slowed himself to a brisk walk. He needed to change his clothing. And possibly get medical treatment.

He called a high school friend, Brett Dalry, whose apartment was close by. He hadn't seen Dalry in many months but the two were very close at Loftman and saw each other during college breaks.

Dalry was in public relations. This was exactly the kind of man Bale needed. Bale went straight to Dalry's apartment.

11:07 p.m.

"Whoooaaaa, man. You look terrible," Dalry said as Bale stood in the threshold. "Were you in a fight?"

"In a manner, yes."

"How 'bout a drink?"

"That'd be wonderful. How are you?"

"Getting ready to head over to Halligan's. It's Berkeley's birthday."

"Oh, yes."

Dalry was in the bathroom tweezing his brow. Dalry's parents were artists. His father, a sculptor, was also independently wealthy. His mother had three famous paintings, one of which recently sold to a private collector for an undisclosed sum that was rumored to be in the seven figures.

"Beer?"

"Scotch."

"Done," Dalry said, swaggering off into the kitchen. "I imagine there is a story?"

"Definitely. And it shall be yours. I just need a change of clothes and a shower and some bandages."

"Anything for you, Balfour."

They walked up the stairs with their tumblers and stepped onto a patio so Bale could smoke.

Bale then took a shower and when he came out there were a pair of jeans and a button-down shirt folded on a stool outside of the bathroom.

Dalry brought some swabs and alcohol and applied it to Ballon's back.

"Jesus, she really went to town on you," Dalry said, laughing as he worked.

"Didn't notice at the time, alas."

4:23 a.m.

After a few hours at two Lincoln Park bars, Ballon was staggering back to his apartment, limping down the walking path hugging Lake Michigan.

Gaggles of birds chirped in anticipation of sunrise. A pigeon nibbled asphalt. Ahead of him was the neon-red sign of the Drake Hotel.

He turned onto Elm Street and walked between the mansions and the trees.

His apartment was dark except for counter-top lighting and the glow of streetlights. He removed his shoes and wallet and pulled a stick from a fresh pack of Parliaments. He walked to the bay window and lit it.

He collapsed into a leather chair overlooking the lake.

He heard occasional delirious noises such as sick laughter and group gabbing and taxi horns that erupted from the monied wasteland of State and Rush.

He dreaded the time he had to spend at home by himself. The little noises and whispers seemed like some slouching beast lurking in the shadows.

Sometimes before he went to bed, the constriction in his chest seemed like it would finally overwhelm him and he would take two or three long rips from a vape pen loaded with 100% indica and flip through the hundreds of vapid cable channels.

Or he would take a swig of cough medicine and swaddle himself in blankets.

He decided to do both and passed out on the floor.

· · · · ·

Two weeks later. Oct. 9, 2019. Inside Bale's cubicle at the bank.

9:07 a.m.

He popped an Adderall XR and set to the tasks.

12:06 p.m.

He and Fredricks filled every surface of the new analyst's cubicle with tiny paper cups filled with water. They got Sherry to walk the newest analyst—an irritatingly dapper-dressed Peter Beardsley—back from the copy room so that Fredericks could snap a candid shot of him seeing the rows of more than one hundred touching Dixie cups.

Beardsley looked like he might cry as he removed the cups one by one while the bullpenners prodded and threatened him.

5:15 p.m.

Fredericks, Rothkauf, and McAllister had encircled a trio of women lawyers from Kirkland & Ellis at a young professionals networking event. Bale joined them after getting a cocktail.

Fredericks was already thoroughly inebriated

("watch how papa gets outta the gates, kids," he had said as he chugged his first vodka martini), and was regaling them with stories of shooting beer bottles launched off abandoned buildings in a forlorn corner of his Dubuque hometown.

Bale leaned close to a Kirkland partner.

"I was just going out for a cigarette."

"Oh, well, I am leaving soon, too."

"Bale," he said, extending his palm.

"I can see that on your name tag," she said. "Jill," she said, pointing to hers.

He was mesmerized by her fishnet stockings and black boots.

"You are a lawyer?" he asked.

She smirked at him, deliciously.

"Listen, I want to ask you something, but you *can't* tell your friends what it is. Agree?"

"Ok."

"Promise?"

"Mhhm."

"You have to say, 'I promise.'"

"Ok. I promise."

She leaned in and whispered into his ear: "Do you like pussy?"

His eyes flared.

"Um, *yes*, I like it."

"No, no," she said. "You don't like it. You *love* it."

She snatched his iPhone, texted herself and handed it back.

"Text me in an hour," she said over her shoulder as she walked off.

The next hours were not good health-wise for young Bale.

Two shots of Patron backed by cocaine key-bumps in a bathroom stall with McAllister and Fredericks.

McAllister had then raged at the "fucking coat-check girl" dirtying his Hugo Boss suit jacket.

Ratcliffe called him a pig and McAllister lunged at him.

Cigarette.

Argument over their next destination.

Stumbling, teetering, urinal-stabilized text messaging to Jill, the Kirkland & Ellis principal.

Receives confirmation of rendezvous, scheduled in one hour.

Cigarette.

More coke in stall with McAllister and Fredericks.

Half-conscious cab ride to apartment.

Cigarette.

Voice-activated speaker activation. Playlist: Jimi Hendrix.

Recognizes nose is bleeding—gets in shower. Forgets he is wearing clothing. Removes clothing while in the shower.

Knock at the door. It's Jill.

Bale: apologizes for answering it naked.

She: "Not at all. Saves me time."

Kissing, fondling, groping.

Asks Jill to perform a strip tease while leaving on the fishnets.

She does.

They fuck.

Cigarette.

"You're fun," she said.

He lights a cigarette and lays down on the bed with her.

He snuggles against her bosom.

He cries.

Wonders what normal people do with their evenings.

Jill says she needs to leave but that he should call her.

He gets up, naked, and walks to the front closet to retrieve her coat.

Said coat isn't fully attached to its hanger, which is of the thin, bullshit dry cleaner variety and can't support his teetering body.

He falls into the closet. Passes out.

Awakes. Darkness.

Jill is gone.

His head hurts.

He looks at his watch—

7:29 p.m.—

"Fuck."

He remembers he had a flight to New York that evening, which he missed, to see his friend Brad Katzman.

Dresses.

He remembers leaving his Tumi weekend bag packed for the trip at the office.

Fuck it, he'll buy whatever he needs.

Gets an Uber to Midway.

Pays for one-way, first-class ticket on the 9:40 p.m. to LaGuardia: $880.

Boards the plane and immediately passes out in his seat.

12:34 a.m.

Manhattan.

Brad Katzman's "it's close to everything" apartment two blocks from the Flatiron.

"Katzman!"

"Yao, Balfour!"

Several Jewesses with large earrings and flowy dresses sip vodka tonics; a couple hipsters smoke cigarettes around the coffee table. Bluetooth hip-hop. Place looked like Bale's. Mass-produced furniture. Efficient.

Welcome shot of tequila.

"Cheers."

Urinates, washes face, changes.

Beers.

Guests take turn snorting fat rails of cocaine off an American Psycho DVD case.

1:45 a.m.

They flagged a limousine on Fifth Avenue. Katzman haggled down the price to fifty dollars per person and four of them got in.

The limo glided through traffic. They hadn't seen each other in months, yet they rode in silence. Nothing mattered. The world is a festering pile of shit made that way by people like them. They used their own self-concocted images to propel themselves deeper into their myth of American success.

The limousine stopped outside a small bar at the end of some craggy street lined with warehouses and dumpsters. They had cigarettes while the girls slipped inside.

"Are you seeing anyone?" Katzman asked Bale.

"No."

"I am not either," Katzman said. "I don't think I am capable of a relationship now. I am a little insane."

Inside the bar, Brad, Brad's friends and Bale took shots of tequila and sniffed cocaine off the slender divot of Brad's BMW key in the bathroom. They reemerged, ordered beers, and took a place at the bar.

Katzman and Bale finally began talking in their mutual language: specious finance. Erotic marketing materials. Salary-doubling bonuses. They talked about Morgan Stanley and Brad getting Bale an interview. It was *paramount* to introduce Bale as soon as possible to a specific M.D. with whom Katzman was on excellent terms. Could he maybe fly in next week for a lunch? As they hashed out the logistics, two new girls popped into their conversation.

One girl said she knew Katzman from high school and her friend insisted on laughing nervously in Bale's face every time her friend talked.

Bale snarled at her.

"Whoa, man, that girl is a friend of my sister's," Katzman said. "What's wrong with you?"

"Nothing. I just need another bump."

"No, no. Have some water. Calm down."

Katzman called for the bartender.

"*Bale*, I am going to get you some water."

Katzman returns. Bale chugs the water, fades in and out.

Pull it together. Pull it together.

"Look at *that chick*," Brad said. "I think I went to summer camp with her."

Bale cleared his throat. "You should say 'Hi.'"

Katzman walks over to her. Bale tries to compose himself on a stool.

"Bale?!"

"Meta?"

"Oh my God, it is so good to see you, how are you?"

"Who are you here with?"

"Friends. Over there—did you see Tom and Beth? Her eyes flicker: "You OK?"

"Of course I am. I have always been."

"Oh, is that Brad? Brad!" She waved. "Hey!"

"Wow. Meta. What a surprise!"

They embrace.

"London reunion!"

"I saw your review in the Times," Katzman said. "What is that, your fifth? Mazel tov."

Bale watched Brad touch her flesh. "That's *so cool.*"

Bale decided there was clearly something going on between them.

He decided they were disparaging him in some secretive way.

He shoved Katzman's shoulder.

"What the fuck, man!?" Brad said.

Outside. Cigarette. Fumbling.

Ow! Fuck. God damn meteoric embered match head.

Bale sat down on a little bench outside the club. He was muttering frenetic airless sentences, running his hands through his mangled hair. His collar was soaked. His eyes, volcanic.

"You can't have your drink out here, sir."

Pause.

Action: hurled glass crashes in the street. The bouncer rushed at him. Grabbed his collar.

"Do I need to call the police, asshole?"

"Fuck off."

"Man, *get the fuck outta here,*" the bouncer said, craning over him.

Bale stood up, teetered. He made a serious attempt to shove the bouncer with both hands.

The bouncer reacted by swinging his meaty fist into Bale's nose. A cartilage crack resounded; Bale saw a blackness flecked with stuttering red spots. He stumbled, dropped into the street.

When he got up, he saw pebbles and glass were stuck in his palms. He felt blood dribbling down his face. A train horn screamed in his ears.

He went back after the bouncer. He swung a coiled fist hard at the man and grazed his ducking ear. The man threw another fist slab that connected with the side of Bale's mouth, splitting it open. Blood poured from it.

He was numb; the earth spun, blinking. He collapsed into the gutter.

Meta saw nearly the entire episode, standing slackjawed beside Brad and a gaggle of onlookers.

Katzman rushed toward Bale, wrapped his arm around Bale's ribcage, and lifted him up. Bale spat blood, murmured. They limped together toward Brad's limo, idling under the bridge about a block away.

As they hobbled by the bouncer, Bale screamed, "Fuck you, you fucking cocksucker!"

Meta, who had been walking just behind them, stopped cold.

She was standing rigid in the street roughly ten yards back, tears slipped down her cheeks. Disbelief over his violence.

Katzman's apartment was silent. It smelled of luxurious perfume and Clorox. Ballon, fully conscious now but still keyed up with testosterone and stimulant, ambled to the fridge and took out a beer and pressed it to his forehead. He slumped into the couch.

Katzman paced about saying, "Jesus Christ, man, Jesus Christ."

After a few minutes, Brad snorted a line off the DVD case on the coffee table and put on some reggae. He made a call and returned to the living area. He sat on a chair and looked at Bale.

"This is a fucking outrage," Katzman said. "We are going to sue that fucking bouncer and the bar. You want to go into the bar business? Because you and I are going to fucking *own* that place."

Katzman suddenly noticed that Ballon had passed out.

The apartment was dark when Bale awoke. Small shadows danced on the walls above the bed. Through the blinds, bars of light slashed over his chest and walls. He instinctively looked at his watch—but it was broken, its face cracked.

He squinted in the direction of the bed. He saw a great tangling of bodies, a symphony of groping and moaning and giggling, and heard the deep thrust of Brad's voice giving directions amid the flailing limbs. The sheet, a big, white, grotesque apparition, danced over them.

He made out the little thrusts of Katzman's pelvis and a ponytail draped over the mattress edge. He saw her angled rising body, tending, touching, and moving over to the other two.

He heard a euphoric climax.

The sheet was ripped off, then, by Katzman, who was naked and kneeling on the bed, sweating and wild-haired: the women moaned and laughed—one reached out and spanked his butt.

"You're awake," he said to Bale.

Bale tried to smile but was limited by pain. His mind flashed to Meta's horrified face, fragmented memories of the night. He faded in and out.

"That's my friend. He had a terrible night."

The women cooed and slouched and slid along the bed toward Bale. He felt horribly sick and demented and pleonexic and his mind lashed itself with anguish and regret and self-hatred. He tried to speak as the naked glowing bodies slithered toward him.

Then he felt one woman's fingers slide along the lines of his pant leg and felt the other's breath on his forehead.

Bale envisioned his death, monied and alone.

· · · · ·

Legible excerpts from the medical notes of Dr. Phillip Fischman, ophthalmologist, for patient #2115/Ratcliffe:

October 12, 2019:

Chief complaint: Bouncer punched patient in OS 2 days ago during street fight. HPI Complains of pain, swelling, redness, decreased vision. Also complains of nose pain. Nose broken. (Diagnosed by X-ray).

Exam: visual acuity 20/20 OD. 20/100 OS. Visual field: normal OD, superior field loss OS. Pupils normal. Intraocular pressure (IOP): 17 OD, 22 OS. Motility: eyes straight in all positions of gaze, full movement OU. Orbital rim intact OU. OD external, anterior and posterior exam normal. OS lids swollen shut with edema and ecchymosis. Mild conjunctiva injection. Slight corneal haze. Anterior chamber 20-percent hyphema. Iris normal. Lens clear. Fundus exam OS: retinal detachment inferior.

Impression: OS Black eye, hyphema, retinal detachment.

Plan: Ice pack to eye, Atropine eye drops twice a day, Prednisolone eye drops every 2 hours OS, oral Prednisone (60 mg) daily, referral to retina surgeon for retinal detachment surgical repair. Dr. Lipshitz.

NOTE 10.19.18: Report from Lipshitz retinal detachment treated successfully with scleral buckle procedure. Restricted activity for 2 weeks. Patient asked if he "could still work." Eye will be swollen and red for roughly two months—ideally: daily improvement. Must schedule multiple follow-up appointments for the next six weeks or so.

· · · · ·

November 5, 2019. Thursday.

8:13 a.m.

Ballon exited his cab at Wells and Van Buren. He used his forefinger to push the bridge of his glasses higher up on his nose.

His vision was limited to his right eye on account of a very embarrassing patch stretched over his left eye, required for two weeks after the post-NYC fight "scleral buckle" procedure, as noted by Dr. Fischman.

With his vision half corrected and his visual plane widened by the glasses, he now took in an increased array of structures and people in his field, seeing, for example, that the homeless man ahead of him, at the corner, had a new sign: "My Name Is Matthew Billford. I Need Food/Money Until Job Secured. Thank you."

Ballon observed that Billford had on a relatively clean pair of brown penny loafers, his button-down shirt tucked into belt-less khakis.

When Ballon got up to him to give him money, the man said "hello" to him. Ballon asked him about his job prospects, citing the sign, and the man talked with pride about "turning a corner" and about a few pending job applications.

Ballon wished him "all the best" and put five dollars in the man's paper coffee cup.

"You look like you got into a bit o' trouble yerself," the man chuckled.

"Corrective surgery," Ballon said. "What's your story?"

"One day I'm comin' home from work on the train and I get this call from the police. My wife and kids were driving on I-94, going home and...[pauses, gathers himself]..."and their car was hit by a drunk driver. Smashed into the median. They were killed instantly, didn't suffer, the police told me."

"I'm sorry."

The man shook his head vacantly.

"I started drinking. Didn't take me a month to get up to a fifth of vodka a day."

Bale watched the cold gray face of the man, his sloppy mouth trembling slightly, his big lashes laboriously rising and falling over his squishy eyes. His fingers strangled the edges of his sign.

"It's amazing how fast you can fuck your life up," Bale said.

"That's true," Billford said. "But look, I'm sober now for six months."

At his desk, Ballon was working on a valuation model for a company Goldman & Coli was selling when McAllister stopped by. The eye patch was now—already—an afterthought. No longer extreme, socially disconcerting, or intriguing—it was fully integrated into the office environment.

"How goes it?" McAllister said.

Ballon flipped through his composition book looking for notations on cash flow.

"OK, OK. You?"

"Yeah. For the call at two, I need you to update the Marketing Status Update. I think Wynnchurch is a 'decline' and that firm in Bollington, um... "

"Omnia?"

"Yeah. Put them under reviewing memorandum for now. Check the database and go through all the contacts assigned for Matrix and check for updates. Make sure they are all reflected accurately. That is for Cross. Second, here is Omnia's CA—forge Cross's signature and scan it. Send them soft copies of memo, teaser, CA—FedEx tonight. I talked to that fucking prick at Carlisle—they declined. Note that on the Marketing Status Update as well."

McAllister left Ballon's cubicle, then spun on his heels.

"One more thing. Update the LTM data for July numbers. I want to show the incremental increase in EBITDA. Cross gave me the audited financials"—hands him a pile of documents—"update that in the model and then print before the call. Alright, man, thanks."

4:07 p.m.

He went outside for a cigarette.

The afternoon rush had just started, and he

watched the trickle of workers eagerly pouring out of the towers toward their briefly non-corporate lives.

His hands shook as he smoked; he felt that the gray blanket of sky might just come down and smother him.

For a change of scenery, he walked around the corner and went to see his homeless friend.

Billford was lying on the little grass plot, sleeping. Bale approached, recycling in his mind the story of the man's life collapsing.

What could he do for this man? What would *matter*?

He stood up and walked briskly back to the building's entrance, nervously smoking at his cigarette.

7:25 p.m.

Fredericks stopped in his cubicle. He tossed a tie on Ratcliffe's desk.

"What's this?"

"Knew you'd forget, little guy. We have the company-sponsored fundraiser tonight. Standard Club."

"Thanks."

There was something in Bale's facial wincing, his pressurized frown, the vacant lull of his mirthless eye beside his grotesque eye patch that worried Fredericks beyond merely the bad impression Bale would give the philanthropists, should anyone interact with him beyond the standard scripted self-promotional careerism that Bale had learned to handle expertly.

So when it was clear that all the directors had left and it was only the bullpen shooting off last-minute emails and the finishing touches on the evening's deadlines, Fredericks returned to Bale's cubicle with a bottle of Johnny Walker Black Label and filled two little glasses with a single cube of ice apiece.

"Walk with me, Bale."

Bale followed Fredericks to the conference room.

Bale went in first and took a seat. Fredericks closed the door and sat down across from him. He slid the glass over to him and they both took sips.

"Listen, little fella. I care about you. You're a great kid. I am sitting here as your friend, not your boss."

"OK."

"Are you *OK*?"

Bale exhaled and shifted himself. He looked at Fredericks' face, which was compressed and emotionless.

"I mean—apart from getting your face bashed in—I have noticed you've been off-kilter. More than to be expected anyway for an analyst."

Bale tried not to move.

"We have all noticed it lately—even the Hurricane said something."

"Goldman?"

"No, no," Fredericks lied.

"OK," Bale said, pretending to believe him.

Fredericks took another drink.

"Look, I am not really *saying* anything by this...

but why don't you take a weekend off?"

"I don't have much work to do this weekend anyway."

"No, no. Not just with work. Why don't you" [he exhaled sharply] "not do anything this weekend? Just stay at home, watch the Godfather trilogy, order deep-dish."

"Noted," was the stupid thing Bale said. "Thanks."

"No problem. Look, do what I say. Turn your phone off, don't do anything. Don't *drink* anything. Don't *take* anything. You know, *relax*."

They both swallowed the remaining liquid and returned to the bull pen, where the men had gathered.

"Where were you two homos?" McAllister asked.

Bale rolled his eyes and brushed past him.

During the walk from the Willis Tower to the Standard Club, the men and Sherry, giddy to have an evening free, were involved in a rapid conversation Bale couldn't follow. He walked a step behind them, listening to the laughs, affirmations, and playful skepticisms dotting their speech—like a film director watching actors behind a camera.

Before they turned the corner onto the Club's narrow street, Bale turned and looked upwards for several seconds at the Willis' silver antennae piercing the night sky.

The others were now many steps ahead of him and he decided that this was perfectly OK.

11:17 p.m.

Bale and Sherry escaped the fundraiser under cover of darkness, after a covert, pre-arranged meet up by the potted plants in the Standard Club's lobby. The plan was to return to the office, where in a giddy drunken trance their laughter echoed off the walls as they shuffled past the fake floor plants, awful paintings, and bulky metal cabinets toward the bullpen.

Bale launched Spotify at his cubicle while Sherry disappeared into the kitchen, soon emerging with one of the shitty bottles of champagne Escher gave each "team member" who worked on the Lazarus deal.

She pushed him playfully and flitted away deeper into the corporate labyrinth.

He picked a song, and then shot around the cubicle wall after her, peeping into different offices, down the different aisles, and then caught her scurrying down another corridor towards the back conference room, where she slipped inside.

The booming crack of Franki Valli poured from the Sonos system: *Sheeeery, Sheerry baby...Sheeeery, Sheerry baby...*

He saw her faint silhouette flick the lights off as he approached the room.

Shaa-haa-haaaaarie bayaybeeee (Sherry Baby)... Shaa-hada-haaaaaarie can you come out tonight? ...

He play-jumped into the room but was startled by the POP of the champagne cork. When he turned to the sound, he got a cold spray to his face and shirt. After flinching, he rushed to her and slid his arms around her back and kissed her.

As Sherry worked her lips over Bale's neck, he tilted the bottle endwise and took a long slug, the Champagne dribbling down his jaw onto the cream-colored carpeting.

Sheeeery...Sheeeery baby... Sheeeery, Sheeeery baby...

He pushed her wet hair away from her eyes and behind her ears and kissed from her lobe down to her neck, her shoulders and chest line and ran his hands around the hugging satin of her dress.

(Why don't you come out) To my twist party ... (Come out) Where the bright moon shines...

They attacked each other's lips and Sherry went for his black belt and zipper and she pulled down his trousers and boxers.

"Lift my dress."

She shimmied onto the desk.

He brought himself into her and they moved in unrestrained unison on the desk for two dozen or so thrusts until they heard a riotous "WHAT THE FUCK?!" screamed by Escher Coli who had flicked on the conference room lights and saw Sherry's legs coiled around Bale's waist and yelled "O MY GOD. *Bale*? *Sherry*!?"

Bale and Sherry separated, though he tripped over the waste can and toppled to the ground. He covered himself with their hands, while Sherry tugged her dress down over her loins.

Escher had hoisted his arms in a huge X over his eyes, saying "Oh my God" repeatedly as he backed out of the room, yelling: "We'll deal with this in the morning."

And he stomped off.

(Why don't you come out)... With your red dress on...(Come out)... Mmm you look so fine...(Come out)... Move it nice and easy, girl, you make me lose my mind . . .

12:03 a.m.

They dressed and fled in silence, emerging from the Willis Tower into a deserted downtown. He walked with his tie noosed around his neck; she walked with her purse swinging in the dead black air.

They were still drunk, but the adrenaline masked it.

As they walked, Bale wondered how he would face the morning, when Escher called him into the conference room, where the managing directors would be assembled around the massive table, blood-red in tooth and claw. And how they would explain to him in stilted corporate idioms and legal jargon what his missteps signified for his professional future.

Or maybe Escher would just fire him outright, gesturing wildly as he told him to "pack his shit and get the fuck out of the office."

He remembered how Fredericks always told him not to try and solve problems on insufficient data, so he didn't.

Suddenly within him a new strategy formed. It was as if two spears pierced and drained the dark bruised night of his festering mind and he could see faintly on the horizon a place for relief.

He closed his eyes and exhaled, imagined the new possibility, let it solidify.

Sherry had flagged a cab and they stared at each other for a few moments through the lowered window. He saw her hand tremble as she put it on the window frame. He leaned down and put his hand on top of hers.

He wanted to say something to reassure her. To crush up the embarrassment and terror his sad wildness had caused her into a little ball and pitch it into space.

He told her that they shouldn't regret this night, and that he knew she would be OK. He would make sure of that.

She smiled at that. That helped.

"But tomorrow will be very bad," he said to himself after the taxi drove off.

A wine-dark sky loomed above. Leaves crackled in the gutters. He barely noticed the stuttering traffic, the little belches and murmurs of the city.

His iPhone buzzed. No doubt a text message from his loyal dragoons yearning to know his whereabouts. Informing him of theirs.

He looked at the device, noted the time.

There was one more train out of the city. He didn't need to rush to make it. The station was just over the river at the edge of downtown.

What can one do after all but put one foot in front of the other?

So on he marched. Watching the tips of his shoes connect with pavement. One foot, one thought, in front of the other.

He crossed the bridge over the quivering emerald sludge of the Chicago River toward the station, in as much of a nightmare as life can be.

AT THE LAKE HOUSE

Michigan: Saturday, November 2019

The four of them sat with their finger-stained wine glasses, destroyed napkins, crumbs, and crusts. They devoured
the roast, drained a bottle of Côtes du Rhône, and
scraped clean bowls now scabbed with salad and
potato bits.

Miles Davis' trumpet moaned faintly through
the home's wireless speakers.

"How *are* your parents?" Ruth said to Sutton.

"O, my father has been expanding his hospice
practice—but business is *dead* [little chuckles], and my
mom is working on a grant for research on paralysis—
it's at a *standstill* [chuckle, chuckle]."

"And law school?"

"Excellent. Our anti-death penalty team has
been a very sharp thorn in the side of the bloodthirsty
Missouri governor."

"Wonderful," Ruth said. "Your parents must be

proud. What are your plans for after you graduate?"

"I'm evaluating an offer from Miner, Barnhill & Galland in Chicago on civil rights defense work and also had a very interesting first-round with the federal public defender's office."

Bale could see behind his refined smile that Bruce was now yearning for privacy with his son. Ruth saw this, too, and took an ungraceful gulp of the last of her wine. Sutton looked between them, confused by the awkwardness.

"Who would have more wine?" Bruce said, standing up.

Ruth shelved her chin in her other palm and lifted her glass.

Sutton and Bale cleared the table. Then Bale walked to the small bathroom down the corridor.

Bruce uncorked a bottle and poured himself and Ruth large glasses and he retreated to the library beyond the corridor.

When Bale returned, the room was empty. He looked out the living room picture window and saw Sutton on the patio smoking a cigarette with a beautiful expression of freedom on his face, which seemed to infect Ruth, seated in a chair beside him.

Bale returned to the kitchen and took his glass toward the library and unexpectedly found his father, who had to put on Ruth's ultramarine reading glasses and was standing at the desk reading a fresh page in Bale's journal.

If Bale was sober, he would have pretended it was Sutton's. But he just watched his father squinting over a passage.

"Anything good?"

Bruce looked up, surprised but unshaken.

"You know," he said, removing the ridiculous glasses and staring unblinkingly at his son, "you're a deep guy."

Bale moved cautiously across the room and sat down on the chair facing his father.

"I have bad news and good news," Bale said. "Which would you like to hear first?"

Bruce smirked. He pushed up the sleeves of his black turtleneck to expose his black arm hair and thick gold watch. His awful expression was scarcely disturbed even as he flicked a tuft of sandpaper hair away from the gaunt desert of his face.

"I know all about it, son."

Bale's grin dried. He was astonished. How could he possibly know? What did he hear? And from who?

"I mean, it's pretty obvious, isn't it? I haven't seen you without your iPhone clutched in your hand in what, six months? And yet, here you are, out at the lake, without it, without a care in the world, writing about *ballet jumps*—he tossed the journal to Bale, who caught it in his chest.

Bale could not make eye contact.

Bruce walked to a chair opposite Bale and sat down, careful not to scuff his taupe boots on the wrought iron coffee table as he balanced his ankle atop his knee.

"*Look*, we all make mistakes," Bruce said, cracking his knuckles to absorb his rage. "The important thing is how we respond."

Bale thought about the past forty-eight hours. About why he fled Chicago and the trail of personal destruction.

"Now, you didn't email Fredericks or Escher or anyone to say you were taking a personal day yesterday? You really just *didn't show up*?"

Vacant muttering.

"Bale!?"

"Yeah. *Yes*. No, I didn't tell anyone. I just left."

Bruce turned his head toward a window. He reflected for several seconds, which was more theatrical than anything as he knew exactly what he was going to say long before this moment.

"You know what? *It's all right*," Bruce said almost tenderly, adding a casual wave of his hand. "You have been busting your ass for that firm. I am going to give Blake Schepp a call and I am sure he would be happy to call Escher on our behalf and tell him that you have been going through some difficult personal things, a difficult transition after college, and that you are very *grateful* to have the job and you didn't want to say anything to them especially in the fourth quarter as they are wrapping up an incredibly successful year."

"Da—"

"—*and* that you will be back at work on Monday morning."

Those last words were spoken too harshly, too

loudly, and Bruce pressed his hand to his shirt over his pumping heart and smiled lightly.

"We will of course take care of this, son."

"But I don't think I can go back, Dad. It just seems impossible."

"Yeah, well. That's *their* choice, isn't it?"

Bruce was about to stand up and squeeze his son's shoulder and tell him again it would all be OK but Bale quickly spoke a pathetic, deflated dribble-piss of words: "I hate you."

And Bruce suddenly seemed to inhale all the room's oxygen as his lips parted and he spoke as if Bale hadn't said that last thing, hadn't even dared to think it.

"Do you know how immature and selfish you are? I mean, you fucked up hugely and I am offering to bail you out—as always—and I am sitting here telling you that I have your back and will help you to correct this catastrophe and salvage your name and protect mine and you don't even think to say 'Jeez, Dad, thank you?!'"

"Thank you! Thank you! Thank you for everything you have ever done for me," Bale said. "What more can I do? Tell me what you want me to do?"

"The fact that it's not obvious to you shows how fucking stupid you are. All you need to do is act like an adult and go to *work*. Don't throw your life in the garbage over stupid pipe dreams. Build your own future. That is all you need to do."

Bale didn't think his own expression was negative, but it seemed to make his father increasingly angry.

"It isn't like you are spraying insulation or cleaning fucking motel rooms is it? Is it?" he screamed. "You are getting paid huge sums of money to sit at a *desk* and do math!"

Jesus, Bale mouthed.

"Oh, am I being unfair to you? Is this too big a burden for you?"

Bale stared frozen at his father, who finally finished:

"I am not going to lie to you and say that I understand your behavior, that I understand *you*," Bruce said at last, breathlessly. "Sometimes I look at you and I don't want to believe you are my son."

Bruce stood up, wiped his mouth, and walked to the staircase, paused, and marched up the stairs. Bale stared at his pages. His body jumped as the slam of a master bedroom door rang out like a shotgun blast through the house.

Bale walked to the kitchen, grabbed a bottle of whiskey out of the cabinet and marched out the front door and down to the gravel pathway, around the back of the house (all this to avoid Sutton and Ruth) and walked down toward the bluff in a confused fury.

The whiskey sloshed as he marched past the apple and pear trees in the long grass. The icy earth swung blind in the air. Across the lake, in the western corner of the horizon, he could see the low haze of the city lights. In the night's cold blackness, it seemed to him to be growing and sucking at him, like an undertow.

He approached the edge of the bluff, where it falls steeply into the sand dune and runs to the beach. He tripped along the ledge, his mind drumming with the events he saw coming that were beyond his control:

Dad'll make a few calls and Mom'll laugh my behavior off with her friends as youthful indiscretion and soon I'll be having a conference room scolding with Coli and Goldman and, after being strongly reprimanded at first, their words will disintegrate into more work that needs doing and new deadlines and then after racquetball and a swim, a steak dinner, angry nightlife, and then the next day's alarm clock, I'll resume the old post, moving further and further from myself.

In a stilted, plopping fashion he descended the dune, his naked ankles sinking into the frigid sand and scratchy grass. He reached the base of the dune, out of breath. His heels pressed into the cold sand, and he raged, totally unmoored, yelling out Virgil like a madman to the atoms in the air:

"Nor can they discern the light, pent up in the gloom of their dark dungeon."

Early morning. Sunday. The dying fire flickered and popped in the trench where they slept in a tent. Bale awoke and sat up in his sleeping bag. His eyelids were heavy, paste-smeared. The scarlet veins of his eye clutched their egg white core.

Sutton moaned, coiled in his sleeping bag, his

face compressed against his fist.

It was just after sunrise, the light coming through the screen of their tent. He rooted around in Sutton's breast pocket and pulled out a soft pack of Parliament Lights, shook one free, and left the tent and lit it off the fire coals.

He walked the beach until the cold water touched his boots. He dipped down and rubbed some icy water against his throbbing temple. The water dripped down his face and jacket.

He walked back to the tent and Bale wedged his cigarette in the pore of a log and leaned down to pick up the bottle of whiskey. He closed his eyes and took a swig, then sat near the fire finishing the cigarette.

Bale's coughing fit roused Sutton who fished out a tobacco stick of his own with his teeth.

"Fuck, brosef, [unintelligible] it's pretty chilly huh?"

"Steelhead are in the river."

"*Ughhh*," Sutton said, zipping up his jacket to his chin.

"What, would a little breeze have stopped Byron? Zane Grey?"

A spritz of rain started. Bale's eyes flickered in the mist.

Bale noted some nastiness brewing over the horizon.

They humped up the dune to the bluff and then toward the house.

"What will you say to your father?" Sutton asked

midway.

"Fuck, man, I don't know."

"You were in quite a state as I was setting up the tent. Couldn't understand half of what you were saying. It seemed pretty bad though."

"Yes it was."

"What exactly did he say?"

"Nothing new."

"What though?"

"How irresponsible and selfish I am. How badly I fucked up. How I owe it to them to get my shit together."

"Does he know what really went down? I mean, could you even go back if you wanted to?"

"He of course knows someone who can get me back in. Repair the blowup."

"*Really*?"

"Yeah."

They reached the top of the stairs.

"Wait. Did you tell him the *whole* story?"

"He fucking knew it already. I didn't have to say anything."

"Whoa. And he thinks everything can be smoothed over?"

Bale nodded.

"Well, I am your friend, and I care about you and I want you to be happy and successful and all that and I do *not* think he is right, nor do I think he is being fair."

Bale stopped, turned to Sutton.

"Also, I do not think you are selfish. I think you

are a good pers—"

"I'm not," Bale said.

"You *are*," Sutton said. "You just need to stop trying to be someone you're not."

They were interrupted by noise on the bluff. They turned to it and marched steadily until their vantage overlooked the great circle driveway and they saw Bale's parents, tight-mouthed and bundled in jackets, stuffing their bags into the Mercedes.

They had obviously intended to stay much longer.

"He should be coming with us, Ruth," Bale was all but certain his father was saying.

Bale hurried to intercept them but watched the car rumble away.

Sutton, who had stayed back in the house to give the family space, held in his hand a note that he found taped to the massive mahogany front door. It was written for Bale:

Bale, I spoke with Escher personally this morning. He said he was very surprised and offended by your actions—you are by no means off the hook, and certain personnel changes will have to be made—but he understands that it was a mistake and expects you to be at work Monday morning. YOU OWE ME. —Bruce

Sutton thought about what going back would do to Bale. He thought if there was anything he could do as a friend it would be to give him the chance to make up his own mind. He crushed the note in his fist and stuffed it into his pocket.

· · · · ·

Sunday. Mid-morning.

Imagine this. This final bit.

They were together, speeding, Sutton at the wheel. Their backs pressed into their seats as the car rose and fell along the wavelength of a crippled two-lane highway, a hundred miles north of the town.

The car was filled with Bale's endless cigarette smoke and bluegrass.

A disgusting ash covered the sky. Drizzle pelted the car and the semi-nude forests. Slicing in and out of the puce and sepia hillocks, Bale saw the rampage of river.

"What about the Scotch, Sutton?"

Sutton's tongue pressed into his bottom lip as the engine roared and the road fell away from the wheels and their stomachs fell weightlessly until they connected with pavement and they lightly lurched.

He shouted: "Eh?"

"*The Scotch.*"

Sutton lifted his brow, gestured to the wheel, which Bale grabbed, and he dug down beneath his legs among crumpled newspaper pages, cigarette packs and empty coffee cups and exhumed a flask filled with 15-year-old Dalwhinnie pilfered from Bruce's liquor cabinet.

Bale took a swallow and watched the river gradually bend away from the road and disappear into the depths of the forest descending into the valley.

He knew every bend of that river—that behind the trees it roared down a series of curves, abutted a limestone wall for nearly a quarter mile, and then opened into a wide, deep pool famous for holding steelhead.

"Take a left at the dirt road a quarter mile up," Bale shouted.

They drove down in the relative darkness until the road became dirt and ended a short walk to the river's edge. They ambled out of the car.

"It is goddamn fucking cold," Sutton said as they strung up their rods and he pulled on Bruce's waders.

"What, did Zane Grey skip the winter run on the Rogue because of a little sleet?" Bale said.

Sutton shivered. Wiped rain from his face.

Bale handed Sutton a box of flies.

They took their packs and rods and the flask and set off down a narrow tractor path toward the river.

Sutton saw the autumnal frost where it paralyzed the naked canopy and smelled the pine musk and hearth fires and heard the crunch and crack of gravel and snapping twigs under their boots. A young whitetail bounded from a creek bed. Mergansers lit out from a stagnant back eddy.

Bale's lungs lumbered, his limbs ached, the liquor dulled his mind. He tried to remember the last time he was sober.

They sidestepped down a hill to the edge of a turquoise riffle, which bent into a wide pool before disappearing into the fog.

Bale started telling Sutton for perhaps the hundredth time how this pool was famous for holding the biggest steelhead ever landed in Michigan, a feat accomplished in late December 1943 by a farmer named Dominic Plume, who used the equivalent of a broomstick to swing a magenta stack of feathers wrapped around a hook into the stout jaw of the giant buck.

It took Plume nearly 15 minutes to reel it in—though that fight, and the fish's 26 pounds, seemed to get longer every year the story is told.

"Thankfully fishing has nothing to do with facts," Bale said.

Bale offered Sutton the flask.

"I'm good, man," he replied.

"More for me, then."

Bale would take the upstream section and Sutton would work downstream.

By memory, he located the row of massive submerged boulders that dotted the river's swollen middle and started out toward them.

Bale was studying the water with a look of absolute serenity, the wrinkles gone from his forehead, his eyes squinting hopefully.

"What are you going to do?" Sutton said.

Bale gestured above the pool.

"No, I mean, if you don't go back."

"What?"

"Say you *don't* go back. What are you going to do with yourself?"

Bale thought of the half dozen driving hours between the river and his city apartment. His real life started to come back to him: his freshly starched shirts hanging chromatically in the closet, the smell of early-morning coffee filling the musty cab while he scrolled through emails on his iPhone, the feel of the office's cropped carpeting on his polished wingtips, his dustless desk smelling of Lysol, the ball of his palm wresting on a luxurious keyboard pad proudly displaying the golden Goldman & Coli logo.

He thought of the emails accumulating in the purgatory of his powered-down iPhone, lying idle back at the house.

He watched the river flow. A smile came to his face. One that wasn't alcoholic or perverse or avaricious—just sweet, toothy, and juvenile.

"I'll take up linguistics," Bale said, grinning. "Neuro-linguisitics."

"*Cunnalinguistics*," Sutton said.

Bale marched off and waded into the river.

Sutton meandered down the rocky shoreline to his patch of water.

Bale felt the water's coldness push against his waist. He pushed his glasses higher against his nose's ridge, careful not to push too hard on his disabled nose and eye patch, and stripped line off the reel and began his cast.

His cast wasn't terrible.

He mended the line. The fly dove through the water column and swung toward the bank until it was straight below him some 60 feet. He stripped in the line, took a giant step downstream, and cast again.

Cast, mend, swing, strip, step.

Bale easily ignored the fatter droplets of water pounding into them and the cold eating at his fingertips and his legs hardening into concrete in his waders.

A storm danced like a colossal apparition above the tree line. A fog thickened over the foothills and forest.

Cast, mend, swing, strip, step.

Thirty minutes passed.

His heart quickened when he mistook a snagged rock for a fish's strike. He shook the hook free, reeled in, exhaled.

He stepped deeper into the current; the water tickled the base of his ribs. He stepped downstream. Shot line. The casts felt better, smoother.

Up the valley, a peal of thunder exploded.

Bale felt a big strike, but the fish wasn't hooked. His adrenaline surged.

"That was a big fish," he said, clicking his cheek. He imagined the steelhead, its belly nearly rubbing the gravel bottom, his tail whipping in the current behind a submerged bolder.

Bale dug in his chest pocket for the flask and vacuumed up the last ounce. He adjusted his hat and pulled the hood's drawstrings tighter to keep out the rain.

He stepped deeper into the current, the water lapping against his chest pocket, and held his arms above the current. He stumbled a bit as he began his back cast and watched his line soar beyond the rod tip in a tight loop.

But, as he watched his line shoot across the river, he caught the sudden terrifying glimpse of a hulking mass spinning toward him upriver. It was a massive spruce trunk twirling in the current after being dislodged by the storm.

He could try to rush the thirty feet to shore but knew he wouldn't make it, his numbed feet like cinder blocks. He could attempt to dive under it, which would fill his waders with freezing water, and he could not judge how deep he would have to swim to avoid getting nailed by the trunk or its spinning branches—what if they smashed his head or hooked him underwater?

Sutton, hundreds of feet away, saw Bale freeze and then the trunk and started screaming for him, taking hulking strides through the water to get back to shore.

The tree struck Bale in the chest, and he latched onto it, and was carried out into the pool. Maybe a jug's worth of icy water poured into the tops of his waders and the added weight caused his numbed fingers to slip off the slick twirling bark.

His flailing arms pumped acid as the current tumbled over his face, the world disappearing into a spinning blackness.

His head had smacked the corner of a submerged bolder. Blood flitted into the water. The trunk nudged past him where a riffle sucked it into a speedier braid of current. It turned sideways and crashed into the bank, leaving his body suspended underwater at the edge of the teal pool.

Sutton had already shed his waders and dove into the river after him, ignoring the likelihood of his own death, and after a half minute had wrapped his arms around Bale's body and yanked him to the surface and over to the riverbank.

When Sutton looked down at him, Bale's skin appeared sallow. His bloodied head lay slumped against the shore stones. His eyes were vacant.

The wind and rain beat down upon them as Sutton drove his interlaced fingers into his friend's chest and yelled his name, hearing nothing back but lifeless silence.

AT THE LAKE HOUSE

Michigan: After it all, 2019

Daybreak. The earth was glistening, gorgeous, and silent.

Sutton stooped over the fire he had built on the beach and prodded the molten skeletal logs with a tree limb. Flickering embers scattered like fireflies.

He hunkered down, lit a cigarette and stared at the fire, thinking of the things he never told Bale. About how hard it was to lug his lifeless body onto shore and thump his chest until his eyes popped open and his lungs expelled river water.

About how he bandaged his bleeding head with a torn piece of shirt and dragged Bale hundreds of feet to the car, where they sat in silence with the heaters blasting, their hands shaking, their lips blue, as Sutton sped him to the hospital. The doctor used a little medical glue to close his cut, and gave him a bag of ice and ibuprofen.

Sutton also never told Bale about the moves

Bruce made to save his son's prestigious job, to offer him a smooth way back to his city life, explained in full in that little note Bruce taped to the house's front door.

There also were the things Sutton couldn't possibly know, such as how Bale would have died had Sutton waited even one second longer before jumping in the river after him.

About what Bale would decide to do now.

Sutton reached into his pocket and extracted Bruce's note.

He read it again:

Bale, I spoke with Escher personally this morning. He said he was very surprised and offended by your actions—you are by no means off the hook, and certain personnel changes will have to be made—but he understands that it was a mistake and expects you to be at work Monday morning. YOU OWE ME.—Bruce

"What do you have there, Sutts?"

Sutton looked up, startled.

Bale laid into the fire a cast-iron skillet he brought down from the house. A chunk of butter hissed around two gutted trout.

"Nothing. Just some trash in my pocket," Sutton said. Sutton squeezed Bruce's note tight in his palm.

And there were things Bale wouldn't dare tell Sutton, either.

About how he remembered seeing the stout trunk hurtling toward him—and on the verge of what he expected to be an excruciating death, he thought of Meta.

He skipped their last meeting in New York and instead pictured her leaning against a garden wall in London, a springtime breeze pressing her hair against her cheek, her eyes ebullient as she smiled coyly toward him.

"Just a piece of trash," Sutton whispered and pitched it into the flames. It turned to ash, an unknown gesture.

Bale understood from Sutton's face it was more than that. But he trusted Sutton at that moment more than anyone in the world, including himself. He patted Sutton's shoulder and walked to the water's edge.

He looked out then over the rust-and-peach-colored nexus of sky light and the lake's gunmetal waves lashing the shore. Wind made rattles of the trees. Waves smacked the sand.

"I should've died," he said.

But Bale was not dead.

Although sadness disabled him, although he was in great physical and mental pain, and although he was inwardly careening through a labyrinth of self-loathing and confusion, he decided to force himself to stop seeing the world the same as everyone else, or as other people told him it ought to be, and to stop trying to shoehorn himself into a myopic slice of America that for him lacked moral coherence and meaning.

The only sign of the accident was the white bandage across his brow stained by a mini stripe of dried blood.

All I have is one life, he thought.

And that realization did not depress him. It freed him. It gave him strength.

Bale reached into his pocket and removed his iPhone, which he had retrieved from its hiding place in the house. He powered it on. Soon he heard buzzes signaling the accumulation of text and voice messages. Dings signaling emails and calendar appointments and conference calls.

As its guts swelled with messages, he read some of their subject lines:

Re: Optimix, for Tuesday
Re: Fogel Pitch_v2
Re: URGENT request for next week—Please respond ASAP

He ignored them, opened the "Drafts" folder and opened one e-mail marked "Bruce."

Dad,
This to let you know I am not coming back.

Mom has told me stories about who you were when you first started dating. She said you were always very serious and organized, but also had a playful wit and spontaneity that she found irresistible. This had a grounding effect on her. And it was that mixture she fell in love with, and which made her want to start a family with you. I won't speak for her, but you have never showed me these qualities since the times we fished together when I was a child. My demand is that you find the will to bring back that man she fell in love with. I'd be happy to join you on that journey, which will very likely overlap my own.

As to your threat to cut me off financially—Do it. Don't do it. It no longer matters to me. The only valuable lesson I've learned from you is that the real freedoms we have are the ones we conquer for ourselves.

B. R.

P.S. When you tell Escher the news, please also tell him that he should give my job—at a higher salary —to Sherry. If he doesn't do it immediately, I'll provide documentation to the Illinois Department of Labor and the *Chicago Tribune* that proves the firm has underpaid her and other women for comparable work done by men, for years. He'll have no problem with this arrangement, I expect.

There was only one thing more to do.

He pushed SEND.

He was suspended. Breathless. Blinkless.

The email was already gone.

It had already arrived.

Bale smiled. He sucked in a deep breath of air, took two steps back, and with all his strength launched his iPhone out across the sky. He watched the tiny projectile twirl, the light twinkling off its glass face, following a wide arc down to the lake, which swallowed it with a faint *gulp*.

It felt as good as an orgasm.

Back at the fire, Sutton congratulated Bale on something he privately never thought he'd have the nerve to do. They talked for a few minutes before Sutton declared that he needed to head back to the city.

"My work here is done," he deadpanned.

Bale hugged him.

"One more thing, man," Bale said, going into his pocket. He handed Sutton a check for $42,500—the exact amount of his prorated bonus—made out to Matthew Billford.

Sutton looked bewildered.

"Do me a favor and deliver this for me? He stands at the corner of Wells and Van Buren during the week."

"What's this about?"

"A clean slate."

And so Bale composed himself. His instincts took over. He pressed his shoes into the wet, thick grass and trudged up toward the house. The wind needled his face. He squinted to it as he marched.

But a smile was on his face—an old glow born of the power and promise of renewal.

There were surprises for him still, such as in the months ahead that his father would feel the clicking choke of handcuffs and the social embarrassment of federal tax-evasion charges, settled out of court for a quarter of his fortune.

He faced down the terror of the unknown, but he focused on the irrepressible love he felt for Meta and whether he might be able to win her back. Such questions are worth devoting a lifetime to answer.

He remembered her demand during that dinner in London—"give expression to what is inside of you in the most honest and direct way you can"—and he decided to yield to the wonderful urge to write something that would lessen the misery endured by his fellow humans.

The sun was rising again, and the beach was filled with the dawn's light, pink and strong. In front of him the path was steep and unforgiving. But Bale was on the verge of a new life. And he ascended without faltering, up and up and up to begin anew.

Citations:

Rainer Maria Rilke, *The Duino Elegies*
Philip Larkin, *Annus Mirabilis*
Sir Walter Scott, *Lay of the Last Minstrel*
Johnny Cash, *Flesh and Blood*

Eric M. Johnson

Eric M. Johnson is an American journalist, novelist, and outdoors-man. Born and raised in Chicago, he now lives in Seattle, where he writes about Boeing and the billionaire space race for Reuters News.

Since graduating from Albion College in Michigan, where he studied economics and English and played soccer, he has written about former President Barack Obama's re-election campaign, U.S. national news, and the criminal justice system.

He lives in Seattle and rural Ellensburg, Washington with his wife and two children, and spends his free time fly fishing and hunting across the U.S. Northwest.